Praise for Ben Aaronovitch's Rivers of London series

'An incredibly fast-moving magical joyride for grown-ups'
The Times

'A darkly comic read with characters you can't help but like'
Sunday Express

'Brilliant and funny'   *Sun*

'From the first time I delved into Aaronovitch's rich, magical
version of London I was hooked . . . I love being there more
than the real London!'   Nick Frost

'The Rivers of London series is an ever-evolving delight'
Crime Review

'Evocative, mysterious, engaging, and, most importantly,
enormous amounts of fun'   *Starburst*

'Aaronovitch has an exceptional imagination'
Fantasy Book Review

'This series has been utterly immersive, right from the start'
The Book Bag

'A charming, witty and exciting romp through a magical
world'   *Independent*

'Anyone looking for an absorbing and enthralling series
that will leave them begging for more need look no further'
SFBook

'Great, great fun'   Simon Mayo, Radio 2

'Witty, imaginative and gripping'   *SFX*

D1428547

By Ben Aaronovitch

THE OCTOBER MAN

BEN AARONOVITCH

This paperback first published in Great Britain in 2020 by Gollancz

First published in Great Britain in 2019 by Gollancz
an imprint of the Orion Publishing Group Ltd
Carmelite House, 50 Victoria Embankment
London EC4Y 0DZ

An Hachette UK Company

1 3 5 7 9 10 8 6 4 2

A CIP catalogue record for this book is
available from the British Library.

ISBN (Mass Market Paperback) 978 1 473 22432 2
ISBN (eBook) 978 1 473 22433 9

Typeset by Input Data Services Ltd, Somerset

Printed and bound in Great Britain by Clays Ltd, Elcograf S.p.A.

www.gollancz.co.uk

This book is dedicated to Lola Shoneyin
because she threatened to beat me if I didn't

Das Leben ist viel zu kurz, um schlechten Wein zu trinken.
Life is too short to drink bad wine.

Johann Wolfgang von Goethe

Komplexe und diffuse Angelegenheiten (KDA) –
Complex and Diffuse Matters

Bundeskriminalamt (BKA) –
The Federal Criminal Police

Abteilung KDA –
The department of the *Bundeskriminalamt*
that deals with the same

1

Potato Fire

In late September, as the nights close in, a strange madness possesses my father. Much to the outrage of our neighbours, he builds a bonfire in the back garden and invites friends, colleagues and, yes, even the neighbours in for beer and baked potatoes. Despite being certain that lighting a bonfire in Gartenstadt is, if not illegal, certainly inconsiderate, the neighbours never complain. This may be because my father is the city's *Polizeipräsident* but it's also because he cooks a mean steak and is generous with the beer. Spiritually my father is a big, jolly, red-faced man who grew up on a farm in Lower Saxony and fondly remembers the comely potato queens of his youth. In reality, my father is a slender narrow-shouldered man from Ludwigshafen whose attempts to grow a moustache fizzled out in the mid-1970s.

'Uncle' Stefan, who came up the ranks just behind my father and has been his right-hand man and confidant for thirty years, once told me that he is the most remarkable unremarkable man who ever lived. My mother says that she married my father because he was the most grown-up man she'd ever met, and if once a year he wanted to turn our back garden into a beer garden that was fine with her.

I've always enjoyed our annual potato fire, especially now I'm old enough to have a beer. Also these days, because I'm older, and police, I'm allowed to sit with the grown-ups and tell war stories. Not that I've got any. Or, at least, none that I'm allowed to tell outside of the *Abteilung KDA*. Stefan tells the best stories – like the one about the armadillo and the Dutchman. Or the time he had to arrest a nun for disorderly conduct.

And the time he found two decomposing bodies in a cupboard – a young boy and a girl.

'Police work,' said Stefan, 'is ninety per cent paperwork, nine per cent bullshit and one per cent horror.' He gazed at me over his beer. He had a blunt face with small grey eyes that could shift from humour to intimidation with frightening speed. Must have been very handy in an interview room back when he was still getting his hands dirty.

I must have looked slightly impressed, because my father got all cautionary.

'Policing is a noble profession, Tobi,' he said. 'But it's still just a job, and you're supposed to come home at the end of the shift to the important stuff.'

'Like what?' I asked.

'Family,' said Papa. 'Friends. The house, the hearth – the dog.'

'He just wants to know when you're going to get married,' said Stefan. 'He's worried you'll meet the wrong case before you meet the right girl.'

Papa snorted but I could tell he was glad Stefan had said it.

'You're worried I'm going to get killed?' I asked.

Papa shook his head.

'"The wrong case" isn't about danger. You only have to spend a couple of nights with Traffic to know that anybody can die suddenly,' said Stefan, proving once again that he was the joyful heart of any social event.

'True,' said my father into his beer.

'So what is "the wrong case",' I asked.

'The one where you go over the line,' said Stefan. 'Where the job becomes an obsession and the next thing you know it's hello bottle and goodbye family.'

Since Stefan had three grandchildren already and six gigs of pictures on his phone that he'd show at the slightest excuse, you had to assume that either he'd never had "the wrong case", or he'd got over it.

'I'll have you know that I don't take my job at all seriously,' I said, which was a sign that I'd definitely had too many beers.

That night I slept in my old room, which my mother has partly converted into a home office. There were wallcharts showing availability and training schedules for the teachers under her administration and, between them, pictures drawn by kids from her school. One of which I recognised as mine – your classic stick-legged, sausage-bodied horse ridden by an equally deformed figure in a cowboy hat. When I looked closer I saw that either someone had shot an arrow into its head, or the horse had a horn growing from its brow.

Cowboys and unicorns, I thought as the beer carried me away to sleep. *No wonder my father worries about me.*

*

I woke up earlier than I expected the next morning and took myself out for a run. The sun hadn't risen yet, but the diligent professionals of Mannheim's most boring suburb were already up and climbing into their Mercedes and BMWs to ensure that they were waiting at their desks when the rest of the office arrived. Some of them had thermal travel mugs containing the morning's second cup of coffee so they could finish it on the move. A Mercedes C-class went past me with a forgotten mug still on the roof – the smell of coffee mingling with the exhaust. I watched with amazement as the mug stayed on as the car took a hard left – perhaps it was magnetised.

I ran on, wondering whether the mug would make it all the way to the office, coffee still in it, to provide a refreshing beverage for the startled driver when they got out.

At the end of my parents' street is the wildlife park which I've been using as a running circuit since I was thirteen. It's a mere three kilometres, a good distance if you're just looking for something to wake you up before breakfast.

I was halfway around when I got a call on my mobile – it was the boss. It couldn't be good news for her to be up this early.

'Tobias,' she said. 'Where are you?'

'I'm in Mannheim,' I said. 'On leave.'

'Not any more,' she said. 'We have a possible infraction in Trier. Get over there and check it out. We should have an information package waiting for you when you get there.'

'What kind of infraction?' I asked.

'A suspicious death,' said the Director, 'with unusual biological characteristics.'

'My favourite.'

4

'I thought you'd be pleased,' she said. 'Jump to it.'

'Yes, boss,' I said, but I finished my run and had breakfast with my family first.

Once I'd given up my dreams of being an astronaut at age seven, a professional footballer at age nine and, in a final crushing of those dreams, a rock musician at the age of fourteen, I decided to be a policeman like my father before me.

I joined the *Bundeskriminalamt* rather than the *Polizei Baden-Württemberg* so Papa wouldn't be able to order me about at work. Just so we're clear, he doesn't order me about at home – Mama does that to both of us.

I ended up in the *Abteilung KDA* because I didn't talk myself out of it fast enough, and because the Director has a vile sense of humour. I ended up learning magic because you can't trust the British to keep to an agreement over the long term.

Mama looked up from her breakfast and took the news that my visit was being cut short with a shrug. She said she hoped that I'd be able to come back again when the job was done. I know he claims to have been scrupulous about returning home on time, but she must have done this with my father at least a couple of times. It's the nature of the job.

Despite the esoteric nature of my work, I spend most of my time in my car. Recently I managed, through some impressive paperwork, to get assigned a silver Golf VI GTI with assorted police modifications. It's dull, but at least it's comfortable and reliable – unsurprisingly, my father approves. Once I'd waved my parents off to their respective jobs, I checked I had enough changes of clothes in my overnight bag, that my scene of crime kit was fully stocked, and that the batteries in the Geiger counter were charged. Then I strapped on my shoulder holster, fetched my pistol from the family gun safe, made sure that my thermal mug of coffee was not still sitting on the roof of my car and pulled out of my parents' drive.

*

Trier is not famous as a policing hotspot, having been voted Germany's Quaintest Town five years in a row in the poll of popular destinations conducted by the *Deutsche Zentrale für Tourismus*. It has perhaps two murders a year and its greatest public order challenge is the annual wine fair. By the time the Golf and I rolled into the Mosel valley and headed south, the Director had texted me the name of my police liaison in Trier. I'd have suspected a prank, only the Director doesn't have that kind of a sense of humour.

My liaison's name was Vanessa Sommer.

It might have been a coincidence but someone, I just knew, somewhere, was enjoying a laugh at my expense.

The *Kriminalpolizei* in Trier were located in an ugly office block right by the train station. Presumably this was so that the detectives, after a hard day on the mean streets of Trier, could commute home to somewhere even smaller and quainter.

Because I was in a hurry to get back to my leave, I'd called ahead. And so I was met in the car park by a stout young woman with a round face, hazel eyes and a mop of brown curls which must have been a pain to control when she was in uniform. My liaison, I assumed.

'Tobias Winter?' she asked and I said I was.

'Frau Sommer?' I asked.

'Yes,' she said, and then, quickly, 'Vanessa.'

We shook hands – she had a strong grip and a strange pattern of calluses on her fingertips.

'Do you want the briefing first?' she asked. 'Or to go straight to the scene?'

I asked whether a package had arrived from Meckenheim yet, but she said no. The Director never sent anything important by email or fax. It all had to be delivered by a courier, who was probably stuck behind an elephant race near Wittlich.

'Why don't we take my car?' I said. 'And then you can brief me on the way.'

Vanessa directed me onto the A602, which runs up the valley and then off onto a newish-looking bridge to the west bank. Ehrang is a cluster of slightly depressing houses and shops to the north of Trier proper, just beyond the point where the river Kyll joins the Mosel. Above the district rose some of the area's famously steep vineyards, with an unsurfaced lane running along the bottom parallel to the railway tracks.

It was good body-dumping country, I thought when we arrived.

A long, low-use lane, with the houses on the other side of the railway blinded by the orange and green sound baffles, and at night nobody would be working the vineyard above.

'A dog walker found him,' said Vanessa.

'Where would we be without dog walkers?' I said.

'Called it in at 21.17,' she said. 'It had already been dark for two hours by then.'

I looked up. It had started to drizzle during the drive over and the clouds were low enough to brush the top of the ridge. If one were sufficiently bold, I thought, the deed could have been done in daylight. Assuming the victim had been dumped and not murdered on the spot. I was handicapped by the fact that the body had been taken away, leaving only an empty white forensic tent behind.

'The paramedics declared it a biohazard,' said Vanessa.

That explained why the pair of uniforms left on guard were standing a whole six metres away from the tent. There must have been one of those controlled panics that evening, as everyone cracked open their emergency procedure folders and attempted to push the problem as far up the chain of command as it could realistically go.

One of those folders had contained the KDA checklist and, when enough boxes were ticked, a call was made to our HQ at Meckenheim and my boss was woken up. That's assuming she ever sleeps – nobody's certain she does. Exactly which other boxes had been ticked to have me dragged off leave was probably detailed in the briefing document that was still stuck in traffic somewhere. The Director never revealed operational information over the phone if she could possibly help it.

'Were you involved in any of this kerfuffle?' I asked Vanessa.

'No,' she said. 'It was a normal day until I got to the office.'

I opened the back of the VW and unpacked my forensic suit, a disposable mask and the Geiger counter. When I pulled on the suit I made a point of checking the seals at my wrists, the Velcro strip that covered the zip, and ensuring that the drawstring of the hood was nice and tight.

'Has anyone taken samples?' I asked.

'K17 did a full sweep,' said Vanessa. That was Kommissariat 17, the section of the Trier criminal police who dealt with forensics. Every state police force has its own way of doing things, and the Rheinland-Pfalz Police obviously liked to have lots of little departments.

I unpacked my sample case, just to be on the safe side, and took it and the Geiger counter over to the forensic tent. Vanessa sensibly stayed as far away as she could without looking unprofessional.

I opened the tent and stepped into the quiet interior.

The body had been found in the storm culvert that ran alongside the road and the tent had been positioned right up against the fence so that the ditch filled a quarter of the floor area. Before I did anything else, I unshipped the Geiger counter and checked the bottom of the ditch – nothing. I've never actually got a positive reading but, as Mama says, far better to be safe than radioactive. Mama used to be a radical Green, which is how she met my father. She assaulted him, he arrested her – it was love at first handcuffing.

There was no body, obviously, but K17 had left half a dozen yellow evidence tags scattered around to mark where they'd taken samples. I followed their lead and took duplicate samples from the same locations, carefully noting the tags and taking reference pictures. It was largely leaf mould, some random bits of slime, and what looked like tiny white flowers. I did find a small blackened lump of lead that might have been the deformed remains of a bullet or possibly a fishing weight. I bagged it with the rest of the samples. Rain started pattering on the PVC roof and Vanessa called that she was going to sit in my car if that was all right with me.

'Sure,' I called back, and finished packaging the samples ready to ship to the labs at Wiesbaden. Then, with the mundane preliminaries out of the way, I moved on to the magical assessment.

The modern magical tradition was founded in the seventeenth century by Sir Isaac Newton. But, despite his work being refined by the scholars of the Weimar Academy in the nineteenth century, most of the basic terminology is in Latin. This was, says the Director, because Latin remained the international language of science – particularly amongst learned gentlemen who never had to wash their own socks. Thus, the trace magical activity leaves behind in the environment is called *vestigia* in the plural and *vestigium* in the singular, and the procedure I was about to undertake was called a *Umkreis-Magieerfassung* – Perimeter Magic Sweep.

Have you ever had a random thought or feeling that seemed to come from nowhere? That might have been a *vestigium*. Or it might have been a random thought or feeling generated by your brain. The first thing you learn when you train as a practitioner is how to tell them apart.

I lay flat on the ragged grass of the lane, let my head hang over the edge of the culvert with the green smell in my nostrils, and closed my eyes. As a general rule of thumb, any magic strong enough to kill a human being directly leaves an obvious *vestigium*. It fades over time although concrete, like stone and brick, retains it almost indefinitely.

And I wasn't sensing anything that strong from the ditch.

For a moment I thought I was going to get back to

my parents' house and my annual leave, but then I felt it. It was quiet and cold, like a breath of wind brushing against my cheek. I thought I caught the smell of the soil and the slow-motion wriggling of roots and sprouts as they struggled into the light.

Not what I was expecting. And slightly creepy.

I got to my feet and wrote down my findings with the word *inconclusive* underlined at the end. Still, I decided, unless the effect was amazingly subtle, that much magic was unlikely to have killed someone on its own. Nevertheless, I'd have to check the body myself. But with any luck our victim had died of something nice and safe like anthrax. Maybe I could still get home before dark.

I found Vanessa reading something on her phone in my car. The rain was hammering off the roof by then and she stayed right where she was while I stripped off my forensic suit and packed my gear away in the back. I was slightly impressed by that.

When I climbed into the driver's seat beside her she handed me a Thermos mug full of coffee, which impressed me even more.

It was horrible coffee, but wet policemen can't be choosers.

'Okay,' I said. 'Where do you send your bodies?'

'Mainz usually,' said Sommer. 'Mainz definitely with this one.'

I called the Director and told her where the body was going.

'I see,' she said. 'I'll tell Carmela you'll meet her there.'

The Director hung up and I told Sommer that we were going straight to Mainz.

'Right now?' she said.

'I can drop you off at the station if you like,' I said. 'But I won't know whether this is my case until after the autopsy.'

'Mainz it is,' she said breezily, but I noticed she immediately called in to get clearance.

2

Noble Rot

The trick with a good autopsy is to try and arrange to arrive just as the pathologist is finishing up. That way you get all the pertinent information while it's fresh without having to stand through all the cutting and gurgling that precedes it. I was aided in this plan by Mainz's deliberately obtuse one-way system, which gave Vanessa and me a scenic tour of the famous cemetery, the flyover by the train station and a baroque remnant of the city's main gate.

'There's quite a good restaurant there,' said Vanessa. 'Or so I heard.'

It was past lunchtime, but neither of us had suggested stopping for food. It's best to avoid eating a meal just prior to an autopsy – even when it's not your first. The smell has a way of creeping up on you and nobody wants to look unprofessional in front of their colleagues.

Especially a senior colleague such as *Erster Kriminalhauptkommissar* Ralf Förstner, head of K11, which dealt with homicide, kidnapping and all the other crimes that make interesting television. He was a solidly built man in his late forties with an impressively long, straight nose and thinning brown hair. He met us in the lobby of the main building wearing a good navy suit and a professionally disapproving expression. An EKHK like Förstner doesn't normally turn up for an autopsy and I wondered which of us, myself or Vanessa, he was there to keep an eye on.

The *Institut für Rechtsmedizin* sits on the edge of the walled garden that marks the boundary of the medieval city. The centre itself seemed to have been built out of enormous mud-coloured Lego bricks. Vanessa said there was parking at the back but it was reserved for institute staff who wrote long outraged letters to your superiors if you took their spaces. Sensibly I found a spot on a residential street further up – outside a tanning salon.

There was a statue on the lawn outside of a woman, hand on breast, looking mournfully upwards as if contemplating the death of a loved one and the amount of paperwork it was bound to cause.

Cast by Irmgard Biernath, a local artist, Vanessa told me. She knew because she'd once had to write an essay about her.

The inside had been refurbished recently enough to have lost that horrible antiseptic smell that can build up in old hospitals, but not recently enough to have a pathology lab with a viewing gallery. Instead, the pathology lab was tiled like a Turkish bath, easy-to-mop white tiles on the floor and green-blue ones on the walls. Around the walls there were glass-fronted cupboards, fridges and laminated workbenches, while in the centre stood a pair of very shiny stainless-steel tables. On one of the tables lay our victim and a quick look explained why the paramedics had declared him a biohazard.

He had been a tall, well-built man, going to fat with

14

the onset of middle age. But you wouldn't be able to say what his skin colour was, because the whole of his body was covered in what looked like short, grey-coloured fur – like the pelt of an animal.

A growth, I realised, like the one you get on bread when it went mouldy.

'Fascinating, isn't it?' said a familiar voice.

Because of the declared biohazard we'd all been required to don plastic forensic ponchos over our clothes and to wear gloves, filter masks, eye protection and pull the drawstrings on the hoods nice and tight.

The voice belonged to Professor Doktor Carmela Weissbachmann, who was the Director's favourite pathologist. She'd trained in Milan but immigrated to Wiesbaden in the 1980s for reasons I've never had explained to me. I doubt Weissbachmann is a real name, but her files are restricted and I know better than to pry too far into KDA secrets. I also almost never see her except in scrubs and a mask, so she was easy to recognise even in full protective kit.

Plus, judging by the way Förstner and Vanessa were hugging the walls, she was the only one of us happy to be there.

'What is it?' asked Förstner.

'A fungal infection of the division *Ascomycota*,' she said. 'It covers ninety per cent of his body but is particularly concentrated at his feet, groin and armpits.'

'According to our timeline,' said Förstner, 'he can't have been dead for more than three hours.'

'Then the speed of growth is almost miraculous,' said Carmela, looking at me as she said it. 'The growth on the skin is also anomalous. I'm not a mycologist but I believe you only get this formation when the fungus is forming reproductive organs.'

She poked the subject's chest to demonstrate the furriness.

'This is a plant pathogen,' she said. 'If it's jumped to humans it would be a major concern but I do not think that is the case here.'

Which was a relief to everyone in the room.

Carmela looked at me again and I think she winked – it was hard to tell through her protective glasses.

'We'll get to the reasons for optimism in a moment,' she said. 'We found traces of the fungus under his fingernails mixed in with skin cells. We haven't fully characterised the cells as yet, but there are marked scratches on his legs, abdomen and chest that broadly match the victim's own hands.'

I heard Vanessa make a little involuntary 'ick' sound behind me.

'It grew on him while he was still alive?' asked Förstner.

'That seems to be the reasonable conclusion,' said Carmela.

For a certain value of reasonableness, anyway, I thought.

'So what was the precise cause of death?'

Förstner was far too experienced to be sidetracked from the fundamentals – starting with *how*.

'He asphyxiated due to an obstruction of his lungs by fungal growth,' said Carmela.

This time I made the 'ick' sound. Fungus growing in his lungs had cut off his air supply. This, I realised, was going to be worse than the thing in Saxony that ate dogs. Still, there was always a slight chance this was a nice simple medical horror and nothing to do with me.

I let Förstner ask the detailed questions. Carmela couldn't say how long the infection had taken to kill him. There was a condition called *invasive pulmonary aspergillosis* that acted in a somewhat similar fashion but that took days or weeks and was mostly associated with people with weakened immune systems. According to the tests that Carmela had rushed through the labs, there was no sign of HIV or AIDS and the subject's immune response seemed normal. Since the cause of death was unprecedented here, Carmela couldn't help with the time of death.

'The initial results from the environment samples are negative for this particular fungal pathogen,' said Carmela. 'But I'm waiting for confirmation from Wiesbaden.'

Who was the next of the detective's big three questions, but there hadn't been much to help identify the body. He'd been a well-fed white European, probably in his forties, blue-eyed and brown-haired. They planned to shave the fungal infection off his face so they could get a suitable image of him.

They had found a tattoo on his upper right arm and already shaved that clean for a photograph. An assistant showed us the picture on a tablet – a stylised laughing face with a bunch of grapes woven into its curly hair.

'Quite fresh, if I'm any judge,' said Carmela. 'It was done some time in the last three months.'

I heard Förstner give a little grunt of satisfaction. A face and a fresh tattoo weren't much, but they were the sort of leads you could throw resources at and get results.

Most detective work, as my father loves to point out, is about the application of correct procedure in quantity.

'Yes,' Uncle Stefan always added. 'Just like digging a ditch – the trick is to make sure you're the one standing to one side with the clipboard.'

'I think that just leaves your assessment,' Carmela said to me. 'I thought the lungs?'

The assistant wheeled a metal trolley forward, with the organs presented in a stainless-steel bowl like the dish of the day.

The lungs had been incised and splayed open to expose their interiors. I've seen lungs before and a healthy specimen is supposed to be a nice pale pink like the inside of a prawn. These were slimy and lumpy and off-white with fungus. I reluctantly leaned forward until my breath mask was nearly touching the pale, fuzzy surface and closed my eyes.

And there it was. Unmistakable amongst the real smells of disinfectant and decay, the wriggling, pulsating push of green things growing and this time a breath of warm air that was heavy with turned soil, and behind it a half-musical, half-discordant note like a violinist scraping their bow down the strings.

I straightened up and stepped away.

'Do you want to check the body?'

'No,' I said.

'Do you confirm the infraction?' Carmela asked for the record.

I said I did.

Förstner snorted quietly. As a senior colleague he probably had a better idea of what an infraction involved than Vanessa. When the assistant thankfully took the lungs away Vanessa asked whether the *exact* type of fungal infection had been identified.

'*Botrytis cinerea*,' said Carmela, which meant nothing to me.

'Noble rot?' said Vanessa. We all turned to look at her, and Carmela gave her an approving nod.

'Very good,' she said.

I'd had enough of potentially biohazardous corpses, so I waited until we were in the anteroom and stripping off our protective gear before asking Vanessa what 'noble rot' was.

'It's used in wine production,' said Vanessa.

'Locally?' asked Förstner.

'I think so,' said Vanessa.

'How is it used?' I asked.

'They allow the grapes to become infected in the fields,' said Vanessa. 'And then harvest them at just the right moment. Occasionally they infect them deliberately.'

'People like fungus wine?'

'It produces a particularly fine, sweet wine,' she said. 'If you do it right.'

'You seem to know a lot about wine,' I said, which got a chuckle from Förstner.

'Vanessa is our wine specialist,' he said.

'So you're a wine lover,' I said.

Vanessa blushed.

'There's a great deal of crime in our area associated with the industry,' she said. 'Equipment thefts, vandalism, trespass. That sort of thing.'

'Ordinary policing,' said Förstner, putting the emphasis on 'ordinary'.

Despite my admiration for Förstner's ability to insult

both of us at the same time, my brain still finally managed to flag a crucial piece of information from earlier in the conversation.

'You said they occasionally deliberately infect the grapes with the noble rot,' I said. 'Do you know how?'

'No,' said Vanessa. 'But I can find out. Are you thinking the victim was exposed accidentally?'

'It's a place to start,' said Förstner, before I could say anything. 'Why don't you two pursue that angle while we try to identify him.'

Strictly speaking, since this was now a KDA investigation, the locals didn't get to tell me what to do. Not even an *Erster Kriminalhauptkommissar*. But I've always found it expedient to let the local police believe they're in control as much as possible – it saves time and effort. My time and effort, obviously – not theirs.

*

'So . . . magic,' said Vanessa, after we'd done the obligatory and involuntary spin around the historic centre of Mainz and got back on the A60, heading for Trier.

'Yes,' I said.

'So . . . magic,' said Vanessa again, obviously trying to compose a sentence that would make her sound like a police officer and not a ten-year-old fangirl. 'So . . . magic is a real thing.'

'Yes,' I said.

'But it isn't like Harry Potter, is it?'

'What makes you say that?'

'You're driving a Volkswagen,' she said.

'What?' I said. 'You think Harry Potter would drive a Mercedes?'

'Don't be ridiculous,' said Vanessa. 'If he drove anything it would be a Ford Anglia.' Which meant nothing to me – I thought the boy wizard rode a broomstick.

'So what is real?' asked Vanessa with disturbing enthusiasm. 'Vampires, werewolves, dwarves, fairies – elves? There have to be elves.'

'Trolls, yes,' I said. 'The rest? It's complicated.'

'Complicated?'

'There are things, and people, you can apply some of those labels to,' I said. 'But it's not like the fairy tales.'

'I hope not,' said Vanessa. 'Those tales are horrible. Especially if you read the originals.'

In my experience, unless someone wants to get into the details right away, there were always two more questions. Vanessa didn't disappoint.

'What about aliens and UFOs?' she said.

'Not my department,' I said.

'No?'

'There's a secret branch of the Luftwaffe that deals with all that.'

'Really?'

'I don't know,' I said. 'If it was a secret I wouldn't know about it – would I?'

'Oh,' said Vanessa. 'But you've never . . .?'

'No,' I said. 'Not aliens.'

Then Vanessa asked the second question everyone asks.

'Aren't you worried I might tell someone or go to the media?'

'In the first instance,' I said, 'you're a colleague. And in the second, even if you were so unprofessional as to go to *Bild* – who'd believe you?'

Vanessa fell silent as she thought this through. Her personality, I felt, was enthusiastic and spontaneous and these thoughtful pauses were a learnt response. Thinking before you act is one of the requirements of a good investigator, and she was definitely ambitious.

This could be a problem later, I thought. If she starts getting too enthusiastic.

I asked how she ended up specialising in wine-related crime in the hope it would get her off the subject of magic.

'You know how it is,' she said. 'Somebody had been stealing equipment from a number of small wineries in the area. They assigned me the case just after I joined the Criminal Police so I was determined to solve it quickly and make a good impression.'

And had ended up making herself team wine expert, which meant any case involving the wine industry short of murder got assigned to her.

'But never mind that. I want to know if you've met fairies and elves,' she said.

That's the trouble with talking to the police – we're trained to be hard to distract.

'I've seen evidence that they exist,' I said. 'But it's all on a need-to-know basis.'

As neither of us had eaten since breakfast, I finally managed to get Vanessa off this subject by turning off the main road at Argenthal and having a very late lunch. While we finishing our coffee she got some replies as to which vineyards were producing botrytised wines using the noble rot.

'There are a couple, but one stands out,' she said. 'Used to be famous for it, but the winery closed down in the nineties.'

22

'But?' I asked, because I was getting the hang of KKin Vanessa Sommer.

'Restarted wine production five years ago and' – she paused for dramatic effect – 'owns the vineyard on the slope above the dump site.'

'What's the name?'

'The current registered owner is Jaqueline Stracker,' she said.

*

October being a busy time in the vineyards, we found Frau Stracker in the family fields that lay further up the ridge that overlooked Ehrang. These at least had the advantage of being merely steep rather than dangerously precipitous. She was a tall woman in her mid-forties with a beaky nose, thin lips and long light brown hair dragged back into a practical ponytail. She was dressed in an army surplus waterproof jacket, jeans and gumboots, the better to direct her workers around the vines. The weather had cleared while we'd been away and the vineyards were olive and yellow in the last of the evening light.

Jaqueline Stracker gave us the traditional look of weary outrage that you always get from someone who thinks they don't have time for this shit – whatever this shit happens to be. But she knew Vanessa by reputation and so handed over work to her foreman, a young Turkish guy in a denim jacket, and answered our questions with exaggerated patience.

Yes, she was aware of the police investigation on the edge of her land.

'I wondered what all that fuss was about,' she said. 'So early in the morning.'

I asked when she'd become aware of the police activity and she gave me a suspicious look.

'When we started working that field in the morning I could see something was going on. It seemed serious. Did someone die?'

'Yes, I'm afraid so,' said Vanessa.

When investigating a death it's always useful to get that into the conversation as soon as possible. Witnesses take you far more seriously, and potential suspects often give themselves away.

'Were you working that field the previous evening?' I asked.

'Not yesterday evening,' said Frau Stracker. 'We were harvesting the vines in the western fields over there.'

She pointed and explained that they were harvesting the fields where they could use a mechanical grape picker. The vineyard above the crime scene was too steep for that and would have to be picked by hand.

I knew Vanessa was going to ask if any of the workers had been down in the field, but I stepped in before she could. That was exactly the sort of work that Förstner would be taking care of – or more precisely, whoever EKHK Förstner assigned to the job just as soon as he'd checked his shift roster. My role was to surf the normal police investigation and spearfish the unnatural as I went gliding past.

The Director says that my unique blend of creative indolence and attention to detail makes me a natural for this kind of investigation. I think she might have been being ironic – it's hard to tell with the Director.

'He died of a *Botrytis cinerea* infection,' I said, to see if that would get a reaction.

Frau Stracker hesitated as the meaning of my words sunk in.

'Did you say *Botrytis cinerea*?' she said.

I said I had.

'Can you die from that?'

'It appears so,' I said.

Frau Stracker looked aghast, but it could have been an act.

'You produce botrytised wine here?' I asked.

'Not here,' she said. 'Not since the war. In fact we only put the old vineyards into production in the last couple of years.'

'And before the war?' I asked.

'It was our speciality,' she said. 'We'd been making Beerenausleese since the Seven Years War.'

And after the war the Stracker fields, which had always been hard work, lost some of their quality. This was put down to an indefinable change in the terroir – which I learnt from Vanessa later was a vinicultural term for all the factors, climate, soil and geology that determined the quality of a vineyard. The terroir could vary from one side of a field to another and often nobody could agree why.

'Although these days some of us are more scientifically minded than our grandfathers,' said Frau Stracker. 'Though the stubborn old fool never gave up.'

The Stracker winery had continued in production until 1993 when her grandfather, Gerhard Stracker, had died. Most of the vintage was sold off for blending and the winery was going slowly bankrupt.

'Father wanted to sell the land but Grandfather had left it to me, and it was protected under the local development plan,' said Frau Stracker. 'I was in California by then and couldn't do anything with the vineyards, so they went out of use.'

Then one autumn evening she was standing on a hillside in the Napa Valley supervising a mechanical grape picker when the smell of the earth had filled her nostrils and she knew it was time to go home.

'It was a mess here, but I've learnt some tricks and I had access to foreign investment.' Frau Stracker shrugged. 'We're already breaking even. In a couple more years we'll be able to relaunch the label.'

'You weren't planning to try for a botrytised crop this year?' I asked. 'Perhaps in that field down by the road? Perhaps spray that crop as an experiment?'

Frau Stracker shook her head emphatically.

'No,' she said. 'Not this year. I know some growers used to do that but we've never used that technique.'

'You just left it to chance?' asked Vanessa.

'Grandfather said that either the grapes would be infected in a particular year or they wouldn't,' said Frau Stracker. 'He believed in a mystical connection between the farmer and the soil.'

'And you don't?' I asked.

'I believe there's a connection,' she said. 'I just happen to believe it's biochemical.'

'What else did your grandfather believe in?' I asked.

'A lot of things,' said Frau Stracker. 'For one, he believed the family owed its good fortune to the river.'

'Don't you, though?' I said. 'From a climatic and trade point of view?' She gave me a crooked smile.

'Not like that,' she said. 'Well, yes. Like that, too. But he meant we had a spiritual connection to the river – one

that granted us good fortune. He thought we had to sacrifice to it.'

'Oh,' I said neutrally. 'What kind of sacrifice?'

'Would you believe wine?' she said.

I heard Vanessa give a little huff of disappointment.
I don't know what she'd been expecting – some pagan
ritual involving animals, perhaps. I've investigated cases
involving animal sacrifice, but they never have anything
to do with real magic. Well, almost never.

'Did you go out in a boat and pour it as a libation?' I
asked.

Frau Stracker looked at me suspiciously.

'That's a remarkably specific suggestion,' she said. 'Is
there something you're not telling me?'

Is there something you're not telling me? I thought.

'Folklore is a particular hobby of my colleague,' said
Vanessa smoothly. 'If you don't satisfy his curiosity he'll
be unbearable for days.'

'Grandfather used to put a couple of bottles, always
the best of last year's vintage, into a string bag and hang
it from a tree down on the bank,' she said.

'Any particular tree?' I asked. 'Was it the same one
every year?'

'Yeah,' she said. 'It was.'

'Can you show us which one?'

'No!' she said – louder, I think, than she meant to.
'No, I'd rather not.'

'Did something happen at the tree?' asked Vanessa.
'Something non-folklorish? Something we should know
about? Were you attacked, perhaps?'

'God, no,' said Frau Stracker.

'So, what happened?' I asked.

'If I'm going to tell you then I need a drink in my hand,' she said. 'Are you two allowed to join me?'

I said yes, just as Vanessa said no.

Frau Stracker cocked her head to one side in query.

'She's the driver,' I said.

3

Wine Sacrifice

The winery itself was centred around a ramshackle farmhouse that looked like it had once been shelled, possibly as long ago as the Second World War, crudely patched up and then left as was for the next seventy years. This impression was helped by a pair of Second World War style corrugated-iron huts that flanked the yard proper.

The yard had obviously only been cleared of overgrowth recently and long grass, brambles and saplings pushed at the perimeter. The gravel surface was uneven and covered in puddles reflecting a low grey sky. A vintage tow trailer, its red paint bleached almost to grey, sat stranded on its rotting tyres in front of the farmhouse.

Frau Stracker pointed to the huts and explained that they used them for storing all the equipment. From the one on the right came a laboured mechanical whirring – Frau Stracker said it was the grapes being pre-crushed prior to the first pressing.

'The tourists never come up here,' she said. 'So we don't have to be fancy.'

The bits of the farmhouse that hadn't been blown up were made of slate-grey stone while the repaired sections were a mixture of new and second-hand brick. Close up, it was much less of a ruin than it had appeared. The window and door frames were all in good repair and had recently been repainted a weird coral pink. There was a blue and white satellite dish on the roof, with a cable dangling down to vanish beneath the eaves.

Frau Stracker led us to a heavy wooden side door that opened directly on to a staircase leading down to the cellar. If Frau Stracker noticed the way Vanessa and I subtly tensed and changed our positions as we went down into the darkness, she didn't give any indication. The police often meet horrible things in basements, so we tend to be superstitious about visiting them.

Frau Stracker grabbed an insulated control box that dangled from the ceiling and pressed a button. Bare fluorescent tubes mounted along a low ceiling ticked into life to reveal a long, narrow cellar lined with faded peach and white walls. Down one wall stood a row of squat stainless-steel tanks and along the other a row of empty mesh-sided metal storage bins – where the wine would be stacked once it was bottled. Pipes were pinned by brackets to the ceiling with branches snaking to each tank in turn. Much later Vanessa explained that they were part of the cooling system that maintained the fermentation tanks at the correct temperature. In the shadows at the far end I saw the light glinting off the round bottoms of rows of bottles.

Frau Stracker told us to make ourselves comfortable and strode towards the far end of the cellar.

The area closest to the stairs had a desk and a mismatched set of chairs in front of a large corkboard. I took the operator's chair and Vanessa perched on an armchair while Frau Stracker hunted out something to drink.

I examined the corkboard, which I imagined had been hung to allow for the efficient organisation of the work rotas and equipment maintenance schedules which now peeked out from beneath a plethora of beermats, postcards, old photographs and flyers from Frankfurt nightclubs. A black-and-white photograph caught my eye, a jolly-looking man with the sort of big bushy moustache my father would love to grow. He was standing in a pose of forced casualness in front of what I recognised as the farmhouse we were in. Minus the bomb damage.

'That's Grandfather,' said Frau Stracker as she returned with a dusty wine bottle and a pair of long-stemmed wine glasses. She offered Vanessa a selection of soft drinks from the hotel-style fridge under the desk. Vanessa chose a Fanta as Frau Stracker wiped off the bottle, and gave its handwritten label a quick look before scooping up a big wooden-handled corkscrew and pulling the cork with a pop. She sniffed the neck of the bottle and, satisfied, filled both glasses.

'Try it,' she said.

It was white wine, a delicate honey-gold shade. I sniffed it and swirled it around in a manner to make Alfred Biolek proud. It tasted nice, and that was pretty much the limit of my palate – I made a show of thinking about it before swallowing.

'Nice,' I said, which earned me a pained expression from Frau Stracker.

'I thought you said you weren't producing a good vintage yet,' said Vanessa.

'This is some of Grandfather's,' said Frau Stracker. 'He managed to produce a couple of good years in the 1970s.'

'You can't keep white wine that long,' I said. 'Can you?'

'Depends on the quality,' said Frau Stracker. 'This needs to be drunk quite soon but he bricked some up in '33 just in case. Said he didn't dare unbrick it until the French left in '49. I sold most of those vintages to raise capital to restart the winery.' She sipped the wine. 'This isn't his best, but it's better than the stuff you buy in the supermarket.'

I took what I hoped looked like a suitably appreciative sip and asked Frau Stracker about the incident at the wine sacrifice.

Like many, Frau Stracker had gone through a short rebellious phase when she was fourteen.

'To be differentiated from my *long* rebellious phase, which started at university,' she said.

As part of that year's rebellion she decided to sneak back down after the ceremony, liberate Grandfather's 'gift' from the tree, and present it to her school friends the next day as proof of her total coolness. Rebellion being all very well, but popularity being even better.

'You go down to where they're doing the road improvements, where the old house is,' she said. 'You can get onto the island via the sluice gate at the electrical substation.'

I had her indicate the route using Google Maps on my phone – amazingly they had Wi-Fi in the cellar.

'It must have been a difficult walk,' said Vanessa. 'Given that it was dark.'

'There used to be a track across the island,' said Frau Stracker. 'Only Grandfather went down there, so it's probably gone now.'

Frau Stracker had been almost to the far side of the

island when it was lit up by the lights of a passing train across the river.

'I saw a woman walking out of the river,' said Frau Stracker, and refilled her glass.

The woman was naked, pale with a mass of blonde hair curling down her back. And she was rising, as if she were walking up a ramp.

'I could still see her, even when the train had gone,' said Frau Stracker. 'It's like she was lit by the moon. But the moon hadn't risen . . .'

As she stepped up on to dry land, the naked woman hummed to herself. But when she reached where the bottles were hanging from the tree, she stopped and turned to look directly at Frau Stracker.

'It was like she was shining a light straight into me,' said Frau Stracker. 'She said, "Tell your grandfather thank you for the wine. But the compact was broken the day they killed my mother. It is a new age and the old ways have gone."'

Then she took the bottles of wine and walked back into the river.

'Did you pass on the message?' I asked.

'Did I fuck,' said Frau Stracker. 'I ran all the way home and never spoke of it again.'

'Why speak of it now?' asked Vanessa.

'Something has changed,' said Frau Stracker. 'Don't ask me to say what.'

'Since when?' I asked.

'I don't know,' said Frau Stracker, and finished her second glass. 'I think it might have been a long, slow gradual change – it might have been decades. I think I only noticed it because I'd been away so long.'

In California, learning to grow wine in the manner of the New World.

'Who do you think the woman was?' I asked.

'I think she was the Goddess of the River,' said Frau Stracker matter-of-factly. 'Or alternatively I hallucinated the whole thing – which, on balance, I think is more likely.'

I asked if she'd ever met the goddess again. Or even, perhaps, left out a wine sacrifice herself.

'Those days are past,' she said. 'That's what the goddess said. And viniculture has progressed. Apart from anything else, global warming has extended the growing season so we don't need to rely on noble rot to produce a decent vintage.'

She talked a bit about soil management and microclimates, which Vanessa at least seemed to understand. I let her ramble – you can't push people who've had genuine encounters with the supernatural. The BKA did a tonne of psychiatric assessments in the 1960s which the Director metaphorically waves at me when she thinks I'm being too casual.

I personally think we should call up *Tagesschau* and let Astrid Vits announce the existence of magic on live TV. But apparently there are 'agreements' prohibiting that approach – and international 'agreements' at that.

When we'd finished the wine I asked if I could buy a couple of bottles of Grandfather's 1970s vintage for myself. Frau Stracker seemed a bit startled, but she was too much her grandfather's granddaughter to pass up the chance of a sale.

'With a sizeable discount, I noticed. She must have liked you,' said Vanessa afterwards when we were walking back to the car. 'Are we going to have cheese with this?'

'This is not for us,' I said, digging around in the back of my car for the old Aldi bag I knew was in there. 'Tomorrow we're going to leave a little present for the river.'

'For the river?'

'You'd be amazed,' I said.

As soon as we were out Vanessa checked her phone and amongst a string of messages was one saying the dossier the Director had sent me had arrived and was awaiting pickup in Vanessa's office.

It had clouded over while we were in the basement and in the darkness it took us a couple of attempts to find my car.

'Should you be driving?' asked Vanessa.

'I only had half a glass,' I said. 'Frau Stracker drank the rest.'

'You had a full glass,' said Vanessa.

'I tipped half of it while you weren't looking.'

Vanessa was outraged.

'That was a twenty-euro bottle of wine,' she said as we climbed into the VW. 'How could you throw it away?'

'I'm not an aficionado like you,' I said.

*

The twenty-four-hour business end of policing operated out of a different building, closer to the river, than the *Kriminaldirektion* where Vanessa had her office. In the *Polizeipräsidium* was the dispatch room, juvenile detention area, medical assessment room, cells and all the other things I'd joined the BKA to avoid. In contrast, the Kripo offices were dark, mostly deserted and, apparently, in the middle of being rebuilt. Vanessa's office was on the second floor just off the main stairwell. She complained that she had to share with a colleague but I noticed her desk was still much nicer than mine. On the wall was a large topographical map of the Mosel valley with curling yellow Post-it notes stuck all over it. And on a table against the wall was the dossier.

'You people don't mess about,' said Vanessa when she saw it.

KDA dossiers are transported in a bulletproof, steel-lined briefcase, which as well as being heavy have really sharp corners hidden under a thin layer of grey fabric. These can be murder on your legs if you have to lug them about for any length of time. There's a six-digit mechanical combination lock and there used to be, or so says the Director, a thermite anti-tamper charge that was only discontinued in 1995.

'What's in it?' asked Vanessa as I strained to pick it up.

'Would you believe homework?' I said.

Since we were here, Vanessa logged into a terminal to see if there were any case-relevant emails. There must have been something, because she gave me a sharp look after reading one and then covered her reaction by asking me what hotel I was in.

'The Ibis Flyer,' I said. 'Do you know it?'

'Yeah, I think so.'

'Nice place?'

'I've never been in there.'

Vanessa was still distracted when she accompanied me back to my car and gave me directions to my hotel.

Finally she gathered enough courage to say what was on her mind.

'Tobias?'

I shoved the dossier case in the back with the Geiger counter and closed the back.

'Is there a problem?'

'There's no easy way to ask this,' she said. 'Only a colleague has emailed me . . . And according to them . . . You can do magic.'

'That's right.'

I was going to have to find out who this 'colleague' was and where they were getting their information from.

'Magic?'

'I thought we'd already had this conversation.'

'That was about fairies and werewolves,' said Vanessa. 'My source says you can actually cast spells.'

'Yes,' I said. 'Is this a problem?

Vanessa was too police just to take my word for it.

'Show me,' she said.

I told her to stand back.

'Is it dangerous?' she asked.

'It might damage your phone and your watch if you're too close,' I said.

'Why?'

I sighed. 'Do you want this demonstration or not?'

She said yes, and stood back, so I conjured a palm-light. This is a luminous globe the size of a golf ball that floats above your palm. It's actually the first spell you ever learn. Versatile and, in this form, relatively low-powered. Which reduces the risk of collateral damage.

Vanessa took an involuntary step backwards and slapped both hands to her face.

'My God,' she said. 'My God, my God.'

'You asked me,' I said. 'And I told you. I even made a Harry Potter joke.'

Vanessa made a strange inarticulate sound common to Germans who've figured out how to start a sentence but don't know how it ends.

She lowered her hands and took a step forward and the palm-light illuminated the wonder on her face. Then she laughed and looked me straight in the eyes.

'Fuck me,' she said. 'You're the magic police.'

'It's not nearly as much fun as you think it is,' I said.

But I could tell she didn't believe me.

*

The KDA travel section, which to my knowledge consisted of one old lady from Swabia, had booked me into the Ibis Flyer. It had big rooms, a weird Roman theme and a breakfast that started at six o'clock. The charm of the all-you-can-eat breakfast wore off for me after a nasty bout of food poisoning in Halberstadt, so I stuck to coffee, bread and jam. Then I drove the short distance back to the *Kriminaldirektion* where Vanessa met me in the car park.

Fortunately she'd calmed down overnight and had taken up the habitual mantle of light-hearted cynicism that is the birthright of every well-brought-up police officer. I knew she had lots of questions but was biding her time.

The sun was still behind the hills as we drove back towards Ehrang. Mist rose from the dark river and the green folds of the landscape, but the sky was a powdery blue.

At Trier the western ridge of the Mosel valley sweeps close to the river, save for a notch where the river Kyll joins the main course. There the railway line and the roads split, one branch continuing up the valley of the Mosel towards Koblenz and the other following the line of the Kyll towards Kordel. The sides of the valley were steep and forested, but not cultivated for grapes.

'They don't face south,' said Vanessa. 'This far north you need as much sunlight as you can get.'

We parked next to a derelict house that stood oddly isolated on the far side of the main road. It was tall and pink and probably at the centre of a planning dispute. Beyond was a low white block beside the sluice gate which was plastered with yellow warning signs including CAUTION − RISK OF DEATH.

We found the way across to the island, just where Frau Stracker said it would be, and even the path she'd described was visible − just − winding through the stands of sycamore, birch and oak. We picked our way along until we reached the far side of the island. The railway tracks were clearly visible across the river and there were at least three suitable candidates for the wine sacrifice tree.

'Which one?' asked Vanessa.

'It's not the exact tree that matters,' I said, so we chose an oak with a branch conveniently at head height. I hung the Aldi bag with the wine offering by its handles and pinned my business card to the top where it wouldn't be missed.

We waited a moment. The mist had burnt away with the rising sun, but the air was still and there was no sound apart from the river and the wind in the treetops.

39

There'd been no *vestigia* associated with the tree, but trees are tricky that way.

'Who are we leaving the wine for, anyway?' asked Vanessa.

'The location spirit of the river,' I said.

A dirty red DB Regional train whined past on the opposite bank and I missed Vanessa's response.

'Sorry?' I said.

'Location spirit?'

'What you might call the tutelary deity or the *genius loci*,' I said. 'The goddess of the river – if Frau Stracker was telling the truth.'

'You know this is the Kyll,' said Vanessa, as we made our way back to the sluice gate. 'Not the Mosel.'

'That would make sense,' I said.

'Why would that make sense?'

'Because the Mosel is listed in our files as *"gesäubert"*.'

'Cleaned out?'

'Eliminated,' I said. 'By the *Abteilung Geheimwissenschaften* of the *Ahnenerbe*.'

Vanessa waited until we'd negotiated the tricky climb over the low concrete wall that guarded the sluice gate building and were heading back to the car before asking the inevitable follow-up question.

'How do you kill a goddess?'

'I don't know,' I said. 'That knowledge is forbidden.'

'So how do you know the goddess is dead?'

I sighed once more and when we got back to my car I pulled out the security case, entered the six-digit code to open the mechanical lock, did the spell that opened the magic lock, and hauled out the dossier to show Vanessa.

It was a standard Leitz lever-arch folder in which about a hundred pages of carefully photocopied pages were separated into sections by standard tab dividers.

'Why is it yellow?' asked Vanessa.

'Somebody ordered black but got yellow instead and I suppose somebody else thought it was a waste not to use them.'

I opened it up to show her the relevant pages that dealt with the Mosel, headed with the entry:

```
Abteilung Geheimwissenschaften          --Gesäubert

Deutsche Volksforschung und Volkskunde ---------NR

Volkserzählung, Märchen und Sagenkunde ---------NR

Klassische Archäologie                 ---------NR
```

'What's all this? And what does NR stand for?' asked Vanessa.

'Not relevant,' I said. 'It means that no relevant information as to the Mosel valley was found within the records of the organisation listed.'

'That seems a bit redundant,' said Vanessa.

Explaining this to colleagues is tricky and, frankly, often quite embarrassing.

I told her that the KDA sits on several tonnes of what they like to call 'historical materials' recovered over the years from *Ahnenerbe* offices and werewolf caches. When I get an assignment my colleagues downstairs in the *Rechercheabteilung*, the Research Department, go through the various files looking for anything that might be relevant to the case. If they find something useful they photocopy the relevant pages and compile a file. Then the head of the section types up the list of the sections and notes whether they contain information pertinent to the case.

'Wait,' said Vanessa. 'They photocopy the documents – all of this is on paper?'

'And stored in filing cabinets,' I said. 'Those great big steel ones from the East.'

'Why hasn't it been transferred into a database?'

'They considered putting it on microfiche in the sixties, but they decided it was too much of a risk,' I said.

'Too much of a risk of what?'

'This is all forbidden knowledge that was not supposed to be kept,' I said. 'Too much risk that other countries will know we kept it.'

'Then why are you telling me?'

'I don't believe other countries give a sausage,' I said. 'To be honest. It's like with germ warfare. They weaponise germs for aggression and we say we study weaponised germs purely for defensive purposes. Nobody likes to admit they're doing it but everybody knows everybody else is doing it.'

It was obvious that Vanessa had only just started asking questions, so I put the folder back in its armoured suitcase as a hint. She started to ask whether magic was as dangerous as germ warfare but fortunately her phone rang and it was her boss, Förstner.

She listened and nodded before turning to me.

'They've identified the tattoo studio where our victim got his ink,' she said. 'Do you want to conduct a follow-up interview?'

I said yes – not least because it would keep Vanessa occupied as well.

4

Location Spirit

The tattoo studio was located halfway down Balduin-Passage, a dank mini-arcade just off Theodor-Heuss-Allee, less than two hundred metres from *Kriminaldirektion* HQ. Sensibly, they'd started their search close to home and got lucky with the first candidate. I suspected the officers assigned had probably spent more time moaning about the job over their morning coffee than they had actually doing it. The studio had metal-framed glass walls that had been completely obscured with hundreds of pictures of tattoos pasted on the inside. A neon sign, also attached to the inside of the window, gave the studio's name as *All Art is Transitory* in English. Leaning with her back to the window under the sign was a thin-faced blonde PHK in a sensible black skirt suit – this was Lisa Ziegler. She was there to brief us while colleagues hunted down further leads.

'He came in three months ago with a group of friends,' she said. 'Paid with a card.'

'I love it when they do that,' I said.

His name was Jörg Koch. Ziegler filled us in on the other details of his life: aged forty-four, locally born, he worked for the MSW Steelworks in Trier-Pfalzel, divorced, two kids – twins. The wife and kids had a home address in Leipzig.

'Jörg Koch has a flat on the other side of the river,' said Ziegler.

Somebody would already be heading for the flat, just as somebody else would be checking for witnesses in the African-American hairdresser's opposite and the internet café next door. On the TV a senior colleague is always barking out instructions while the juniors jump to it, but in real life the police already know what tasks they're supposed to be doing next, especially at the start of an investigation. Except for Vanessa, of course, but that was my fault.

'So what do *we* do?' she said.

'Everything else,' I said.

The proprietor and sole employee of *All Art is Transitory* was called Gaston, although his ID card listed him as Dominique Farandis from Luxembourg, who'd been working in Germany long enough to have picked up a Berlin accent.

'Although, oddly,' he said, 'I've never lived in Berlin.'

Gaston was a short, bulky man in his late fifties who favoured tight jeans, studded belts and sleeveless T-shirts, the better to show off the tattoos on his own arms. Only the absence of a mullet or a purple Mohican saved him from a breach of the EU directive against egregious cliché embodiment.

The floor was a clean yellow lino that I guessed Gaston had inherited from the last business to occupy the unit. Apart from a full-length mirror, the walls were completely covered with pictures split evenly between design exemplars neatly arrayed against white backgrounds and photographs of customers proudly showing off Gaston's work. There was a green leather dentist's chair, a chrome office operator's chair and a stool. Gaston had the chair. I took the stool and Vanessa stayed standing, apparently absorbed in the art on the walls.

'I notice you don't do piercings,' she said.

'Nah,' said Gaston. 'I'm squeamish, aren't I? Also it may look good, but it's not exactly art, now, is it?'

One wall had a wide ledge covered in pink Formica that served Gaston as an equipment store and desk. On it were his pattern books, the topmost of which was opened to the page displaying the image that matched Jörg Koch's tattoo. Without the distortion it was easier to make out the grapes woven into the hair, and the mad staring eyes.

'Dionysus,' said Gaston. 'The Greek god of wine.'

In the pattern book there was a motto in Latin – *In Vino Veritas*. I tapped my finger on it and asked why Jörg Koch had omitted the tag.

'He wanted a different motto – a quote in German,' said Gaston. 'But they couldn't agree on the exact wording, so he said he'd come back after he'd looked it up and have me finish it.'

The quote had been something about drinking bad wine.

'Goethe?' I asked. 'Life is too short to drink bad wine?'
Gaston shrugged.

'And who were *they*?' asked Vanessa.

'They' were the group of friends who'd come to watch Jörg get his ink. We asked for descriptions, Gaston complained that he'd already done that for the first set of police, and we asked him to humour us.

'One of them was black,' he said. 'African, I think.'

I asked whether he had an accent.

'Didn't notice,' said Gaston. 'But he sounded like he was from Hamburg.'

We were basically asking the same questions as Ziegler's team, but with a slightly different emphasis. In routine policing you do this in case it jogs the witness's memory or uncovers a lie. But in my line of work you look for a pattern of reactions that indicates whether they've been exposed to the supernatural.

Not that the three are mutually exclusive. Like any trauma, exposure to magic or the inexplicable can cause people to misinterpret reality.

Gaston did betray an abstracted quality that might have been the result of magic. But was more likely down to consuming, I suspected, a tremendous amount of recreational chemicals. When I first started with the KDA I nearly sanctioned a woman in Munich as suffering from possession when it was actually an adverse reaction to hay fever medication. I'm much more careful these days.

I would have done another round, but Ziegler stuck her head through the door and reminded me that I'd asked to look at Jörg Koch's flat.

This was across the river in Trier-West. It was part of a dirty pink four-storey block of former workmen's apartments with its own car park and bedraggled green area. I'd asked Förstner to hold off the initial search until I'd had a chance to assess the location myself. As a result, the search and forensic teams were waiting patiently in the car park – they seemed perfectly happy for me and Vanessa to go in first. Perhaps they were still worried about biohazards.

We ignored a tiny lift that appeared to have been retro-fitted into the block for the use of gnomes and took the clean but worn cement stairs up to the third floor. After a quick breather on the landing we found the flat's front door guarded by a dark young man in uniform.

'Morning, Max,' said Vanessa, and he let us in.

It was a two-bedroom family flat with views east downslope to the river and the town centre beyond. The hall smelt of fresh paint and turpentine and the floor was laid with that fake parquet flooring that comes in rolls. We found more of the stuff stacked in the living room – obviously ready to be used. There was a newly bought sofa still in its protective plastic covering and paint-splattered sheets had been spread across the floor. A row of orange Hornbach bags was arrayed neatly under the windows. Vanessa poked around cautiously with a gloved finger – looking for receipts.

'Paint, brushes, rollers,' she said. 'Those plastic things that you use to hang curtains.'

'He seemed a bit keen on home improvement,' I said.

'And recently too,' said Vanessa, holding up a receipt. 'This was three weeks ago.'

Inside the kitchen, the cooker was a brand new stainless-steel cube but the fridge was old, cream-coloured with rounded corners. The cupboards had all been recently installed, so recently in fact that the cutlery and a meagre selection of battered pots and pans were still piled on a rickety kitchen table. It was a typical bach-elor's assemblage, heavy on tin and bottle openers and light on whisks, colanders and other things you really need to make a decent meal.

As far as we could tell, the only room not halfway

through a transformation was the main bedroom. The bed was old and unmade, although the sheets were clean. There were piles of Blu-rays, tattered magazines, books, two old toolboxes and three cardboard boxes full of random bric-à-brac, including battered Christmas decorations and old chocolate tins. I checked the books.

'Anything interesting?' asked Vanessa.

'They're mostly technical manuals from his work,' I said.

Vanessa found an A3 artist's sketchpad tucked behind a box of vinyl LPs. Half the pages had been used, all nudes, all seemingly drawn from life and most of them terrible.

'I think he was getting better,' said Vanessa as she flicked through to the last picture. 'Perhaps he was taking classes?'

It seemed an odd thing for a steelworker to have taken up.

The most telling room in the flat was the second bedroom. Here the decorating had been finished, the walls painted a pale yellow, brand new white shag carpet laid down and a teenager-sized bunk bed assembled.

'Two kids, right?' said Vanessa.

'Shit,' I said.

We didn't need to wait for the inevitable follow-up inquiry and the interview with the estranged wife in Leipzig. I was willing to bet good money that Jörg Koch hadn't seen much of his kids in the last few years, and that recently he'd made a concerted effort to get in contact. Obviously, a visit had been planned, or at least hoped for. And all the home improvement had been for his kids. Or, more likely according to Vanessa, to convince his ex-wife he was a reformed character and a safe pair of hands.

As police you can live with the violence, the squalor and the stupidity – it's the waste of people's futures that really grinds you down.

But, unless his ex had cast a spell on him, this was nothing to do with me.

I had Vanessa wait outside with Max while I did an initial *vestigia* assessment, but there was just the usual background you expect from a seventy-year-old house. Brick and stone retain *vestigia* well and the mere fact of human occupancy generates a magical effect. Not the large immediate effect you get from a spell or an infraction by something supernatural, but over the years it accumulates. It's what makes houses feel lived in. Some things – let's call them revenants – drain their surroundings of *vestigia*. These things can be hideously dangerous, so if I find an old house without *vestigia* I usually pop back to the car and fetch my flamethrower.

Vanessa called in to ask whether I was finished and I said I was. I was about to say that we needed to find Koch's friends when my phone rang. I looked and saw it was showing a blocked number.

I answered. A woman's voice said, '*Kriminalkommissar* Winter?'

'Speaking – who is this?'

'I'm the one who drank your wine,' said the voice. 'I'll be by St Peter's Fountain for the next fifteen minutes.' Then she hung up.

I ran out and grabbed Vanessa, who was well trained enough to know when to follow a colleague's lead and ask questions after. We ran down the stairs and out to where the VW was parked. Without breaking stride I shouted to the waiting officers that the flat was all theirs and was reversing out of the car park before Vanessa had finished buckling up her seatbelt.

'Where's St Peter's Fountain?' I asked.

'In the main market,' said Vanessa, and gave me directions. Sensibly she waited until she was sure I was going in the right direction before asking why we were tearing across the Roman bridge with our light strips flashing.

I told her that somebody had found the wine sacrifice.

'A location spirit?' she asked. 'A river goddess?'

'Let's hope so. Or that will be a waste of twenty-six euros.'

Trier's main market square is an irregular 'A' shape in the centre of the old city. It and the surrounding streets are all pedestrianised, so we had to walk the last hundred metres. Since it was Saturday morning the square was crowded with shoppers and tourists. At the northern end was the market cross, in the centre a circular booth that promoted local wines, a cluster of market stalls and a miniature roller coaster for tiny tots.

St Peter's Fountain sat at the southern end. The saint himself is perched on top of a slender gilt-and-white column around which were arranged, Vanessa explained later, the four civil virtues: Justice, Strength, Temperance, and Wisdom. Along with diverse beasts to represent their corresponding vices. The whole thing was mounted on a high plinth so that bored provincial teenagers had something to lean against. At some point in the recent past a spiky wrought-iron fence had been built along the top of the plinth, either to keep the teenagers out or the virtues in.

Standing by the fountain was a small busty woman in

a see-through vinyl mac over an oyster-coloured jumper and skinny black jeans. Her dark blonde hair was cut into a short bob that framed a plump oval face, wide-set brown eyes and a small mouth fixed in a disapproving line.

I haven't met that many location spirits, but I knew her immediately by the impossibly smooth skin and the naked dislike with which she regarded me. They all start off like that for historical reasons and the Director expects me to placate them, or at the very least not be killed. She says she chose me for my charm, but I'm pretty certain she was being sarcastic.

Or rather – as Carmela the pathologist once pointed out about the Director – if she's talking she's probably being sarcastic.

By the waiting woman's side was a small annoyed child of four or five, dressed in a shiny red PVC raincoat with matching court shoes. Her hood was down to show black ringlets that fell to her shoulders. She had hazel eyes and an expression that managed to be even angrier than her companion's.

At the KDA the protocol for dealing with local gods is formal politeness.

'Good day,' I said. 'My name is Tobias Winter.'

Before the older woman could speak the child ran forward, swore at me in French and kicked me hard in the shin. It was as painful as it was unexpected, and it was only because I managed to grab on to Vanessa's arm that I didn't fall over.

By the time I'd recovered my wits the child had retreated to hide behind the older woman's legs. From that safe vantage she peered out to scowl at me.

'You can call me Kelly,' said the older woman, as if nothing had happened.

'Pleased to meet you,' I said through gritted teeth.

'Of course you are,' said Kelly, while the child spat something in French that made Vanessa gasp – she obviously understood what it meant. Kelly asked me who she was.

'This is my colleague Vanessa Sommer,' I said.

Kelly's face broke into a sudden smile.

'Sommer and Winter,' she said. 'You're not serious?'

'A total coincidence,' I said, which only made Kelly's smile wider.

The child made a move to run forward again – no doubt to kick me in the other shin – but Kelly prevented her with a firm hand on her shoulder.

'Behave,' she said. 'Or I won't bring you out again.'

'Is your child okay?' asked Vanessa.

'Stay out of this,' said Kelly, and waved her hand. Vanessa's mouth shut with an audible click.

I turned to Vanessa, who was looking puzzled at her sudden inability to open her mouth. She gazed at me with growing panic – I knew the feeling.

'Stay calm,' I said. 'It's only temporary.' Which got me a glare from Vanessa.

I turned back to Kelly.

'Let her go,' I said.

'Or what, my dear *Obersturmbannführer*?' asked Kelly. 'Will it be the *Abteilung Geheimwissenschaften* at dawn? Mercury in my headwaters? Vampires?'

'That was eighty years ago,' I said.

'That means nothing to me,' spat Kelly. 'It means nothing to me . . .'

She trailed off suddenly and I realised her attention was focused on Vanessa, who had her hand raised like an obedient *kindergartenkind*.

'Yes?' asked Kelly. 'What is it?'

Released to speak, Vanessa immediately turned her full attention on the child.

'Would you like a pastry?' she asked.

The child gave Vanessa a long, calculating look.

'Can I pick the one I like?' she asked in German.

'Of course.'

Vanessa held out her hand and, after a long enough pause to establish that her acceptance was entirely conditional, the girl skipped forward and took it. Kelly and I watched them walk off in amazed silence.

'Who's that?' asked Kelly.

'Local police,' I said. 'Nobody special.'

'Yes,' said Kelly. 'But there's special and there's special, isn't there?'

'Never mind her. Who's the child?'

'She arrived about four and a half years ago,' she said.

We looked over to where she and Vanessa had disappeared into the bakery.

'Arrived how?' I asked.

'I don't think we know each other well enough to be talking about these things yet,' she said.

'But she's the Mosel?'

'You'll have to ask her about that.'

'I don't think she's going to talk to me.'

'What a shame.'

'I was going to ask you whether you'd noticed any changes recently,' I said. 'But obviously things *have* changed.'

Kelly shrugged.

'Things are always changing,' she said. 'From my point of view. It was only last millennium that the Vikings burnt down the old market and the archbishop moved it here.' She pointed at a large Celtic cross that stood at the other end of the square.

'Marked it with a cross and later this fountain. Both of them fakes, by the way – the originals are in the museum,' she said. 'I've always been very relaxed about the flow of events right up to the moment when you lot killed my mother.' She gave me a tight smile. 'That sort of thing causes resentment.'

'And recently?'

'Is it true that the Nightingale has taken an apprentice?'

'His name is Peter Grant,' I said. 'And he might not be the only one.'

'And the Ice Queen chose you as her response?'

That was a new nickname for the Director. Usually the supernatural types call her *die Hexe aus dem Osten* – the Witch from the East.

I said that I was that apprentice, hoping to inject the right degree of humility into the statement.

Kelly snorted and shook her head.

'I met him during the war, you know,' she said, growing serious. 'The Nightingale. He lay in my arms for three days under the Roman bridge while the werewolves snuffled up and down the banks. He nearly died of a fever.'

The Research Department were going to love that titbit.

'There's change coming from London—' Kelly stopped suddenly and looked over my shoulder. 'Where are they going now?'

I turned and saw that the child in the red raincoat, with a *Rosinenschnecke* in one hand, was pulling Vanessa over towards the miniature roller coaster.

'Change coming from London?' I asked.

'Nothing specific to here,' said Kelly, clearly distracted. 'But there's more . . .' She hesitated for a moment. 'More of what you people call "magic" about. When there's more of that – *things* happen.'

This I had been taught, as a theory at least. Magic is generated from various sources, and if not consumed by natural processes – such as location spirits and ghosts – it can behave like a supersaturated solution and new structures can suddenly crystallise out of apparent nothingness.

Or suddenly become combustible, like vaporised petrol.

I asked what kind of things might happen. But Kelly's attention was on the little girl now riding the roller coaster, supervised by Vanessa.

'How long do you think they're going to be?' she asked.

'My guess is until she gets bored,' I said.

'That could be a while,' said Kelly.

I indicated the wine stall.

'Do you want a glass of wine?' I asked.

'You think I should have a drink with you?' she said. 'Despite what happened to my mother and my sisters and all that death and destruction?'

I shrugged and said nothing. When you're police, people are angry at you all the time – you learn to cope.

'Fine,' said Kelly. 'I wonder if they have a decent red.'

5

Art Appreciation

The wine booth was run by the Trier Tourism and Marketing GmbH and featured the product of a different winery every few days in rotation. Today it was a nice Riesling from a winery to the east of Trier.

'One of the Ruwer's,' said Kelly.

'And how are they?'

'We haven't talked for a while,' said Kelly. 'Not since the Diet of Worms in fact.'

Because I knew the Director would want to know, I tried to press Kelly about changes in the region. And also the nature of the small child who was currently yelling her head off behind the wheel of a red miniature fire engine as it rolled up and down the smooth steel hills of the roller coaster.

'I can't explain what I don't understand myself,' said Kelly. 'There's more than one of these children, though, and the rumour is that they're popping up all over England as well.'

'Baby goddesses?'

'If you like.'

'And why are you stuck looking after her?'

'Who else is there?' said Kelly.

I switched back to asking about the Stracker winery,

noble rot and Kelly's relationship with both. I asked whether she really blessed their vines and made them fruitful.

'Fruitful?' said Kelly, and giggled. 'Things don't work the way you people think they do. We're just like everybody else.' She gestured at the crowds of shoppers around us. 'If we like people, then we want them to do well. Sometimes good things happen. Crops ripen. Babies are born healthy. Careers prosper. And perhaps that's down to us.'

'And the noble rot?' I asked. 'Is that part of it?'

'Not intentionally,' she said, but she was holding back.

I might have got more, but just then Vanessa brought the child over to the booth. The child tugged Kelly's arm until she bent down low enough that the girl could whisper in her ear.

Kelly glanced up at Vanessa before telling the girl, 'That's not allowed. You know the rules.'

The child pouted and I realised it was time to make our escape.

I said a polite goodbye, explained that we had urgent business elsewhere, grabbed Vanessa's elbow and guided her away from the booth.

'What's the hurry?' she said. 'Where are we going?'

'Away,' I said. 'Unless you want to be a high priestess of a very select religion.'

Vanessa gave me a startled look as what I said meshed with her recent experiences.

'She couldn't?' she hissed.

'She could,' I said. 'Although to be fair it usually wears off over time.'

'Usually?'

We ducked into a smaller cobbled square surrounded by cafés, bars and hotels.

'Some people make a career of it,' I said, and pulled Vanessa into a hotel bar where I ordered a double vodka for each of us.

'I don't like vodka,' said Vanessa, but I told her it was medicinal.

'That was the *Bezauberung*, the glamour,' I said, while Vanessa dutifully drained her shot and made a face. 'If a location spirit exerts itself, then it can influence your actions.'

'And you didn't think to warn me before the meeting?'

'I didn't think she'd try something in the middle of the main square,' I said. 'But it's difficult to judge how a location spirit is going to react. Mainly because I don't meet directly with them very often. Apart from anything else, they don't like us very much.'

'I noticed that,' she said. 'Did you get anything useful?'

'She said it wasn't her.'

'Do you believe her?'

I told Vanessa about Kelly's report that the overall level of magic was rising and how when that happened you get an increase in what we at the KDA call supernatural infractions. Vanessa listened without comment and then ordered two double espressos.

'To counteract those vodkas,' she said. 'And does this mean that, in the past, levels of magic were higher?'

'There was more activity,' I said. 'That much is certain. Why do you ask?'

'I think it's time we went to the museum.'

I looked at my watch – it was past twelve.

'Let's eat first,' I said. 'And give the goddesses a chance to clear the area.'

*

North of the main market runs the Simeonstraße and rising at the far end of the street like a dirty brown and black lump of weathered stone was the Porta Nigra – the Black Gate. It had marked, Vanessa said, the northern boundary of the Roman city. In the tenth century a mad monk from Syracuse named Simeon had himself walled up inside. His aim apparently was to sanctify this pagan monument. Shortly after he started work, the river flooded – devastating the city. The townsfolk blamed Simeon. So did my dossier when I had a look. Still, the flood receded and Simeon kept on praying until he dropped dead and was buried in his sleeping cell. This got him canonised by both the Eastern and the Western Churches, which was probably what he was aiming for.

Armed with this new saint, the clergy then moved in and turned the pile into a church and built a monastery in Simeon's name next door. A thousand years later the Porta Nigra is a major tourist attraction and the monastery buildings serve as the City Museum.

Vanessa identified herself to the museum staff in the crisp white minimalist entrance, led me past a room of statues and paintings, a mini cinema full of fractious kids and, ignoring the lift, up three flights of stairs. The original monastery had been built around a central courtyard with an elevated cloister along which the museum curators had arranged lines of statues.

Vanessa stopped in front of one statue, checked it, muttered something and moved on to find what she was looking for on the western side. She turned to me and gave a triumphant wave.

'Look familiar?' she asked.

The curves were even more exaggerated, but there was no mistaking the face – although the expression of joyful humour was difficult to associate with the real Kelly, also known as the goddess of the river Kyll. The statue was white alabaster and depicted, according to the writing on the plinth, Methe the goddess of drunkenness. She was holding aloft a drinking bowl in one hand and was dressed in about a half a metre of gauzy fabric and wearing, at a jaunty angle, a centurion's plumed helmet.

Wine, religion and Romans – I was beginning to get the hang of Trier.

'So who's Methe?' I asked. 'Besides being the goddess of drunkenness.'

'No idea,' said Vanessa. 'But somebody here is bound to know.'

The somebody we located was a middle-aged woman called Petra with big hair, a starched white blouse and a smart skirt suit – one of the museum curators. She explained that the sculpture had been by Ferdinand Tietz, who'd spent the middle of the eighteenth century knocking out a ton of statues for various princes and archbishops, including that of Trier.

'As to Methe,' said Petra, 'she was the daughter of Dionysus and wife of Staphylus and mother of Botrys.'

'Dionysus is the god of wine, yes?' I asked.

'Strictly speaking, the god of the grape harvest, winemaking, theatre and fertility,' said Petra with a certain relish.

His son-in-law, Methe's husband Staphylos, was supposed to have died suddenly after a heavy drinking bout and his name became the Greek word for a bunch of grapes, while the grape itself was named after her son Botrys.

'We have a statue of Staphylos as well.' Petra took us around the cloister and stopped in front of a second statue. 'Also by Tietz,' she said. Despite being less well preserved there was no mistaking the plump lasciviousness that was the sculpture's hallmark.

'Unfortunately, this was one was severely damaged in the nineties,' said Petra. 'We believe it was a deliberate act of vandalism by French officers.'

I could see the reasoning, because the damage was confined entirely to the statue's face, leaving the body in as good a condition as the statue of his wife Methe. I asked what evidence they had that the damage had been done by French officers.

'The two statues were originally looted from Molsberg Castle and placed as a matched pair flanking the main staircase in the French Officers' Casino in the Corn Market.'

From the smooth way she recited this I guessed that this was part of Petra's routine spiel. There was photographic evidence of the statue being fully intact as late as 1998, but when the square was redeveloped in the early 2000s it was found to be missing its face.

'It was quite a scandal,' said Petra. 'The builders were adamant that they had found the statue in the present condition. Even if they were not directly responsible, the French military were certainly indirectly responsible for the safe keeping of such a valuable artefact.'

As a result it had been agreed that both statues would be relocated to the City Museum for safe keeping.

Staphylos had been depicted wearing what I could only describe as a hipster toga which hung precariously off his hips and left one shoulder bare. He held a bunch of grapes aloft in his left hand and a second bunch at waist level in the other.

'Notice anything?' I asked Vanessa, and pointed at the lower of the bunches of grapes.

'Oh shit,' she said.

With the same skill and attention that he'd shown depicting Methe's see-through top, Tietz had sculpted the strands and fuzz of the fungal infection that covered the grapes.

*

'I'm not exactly impressed with your police work so far,' said Vanessa.

We were sitting in her office back at the *Kriminaldirektion* HQ, which I'd just learnt was nicknamed the Post Office because of the main branch located next door. They'd offered me one of the spare offices on the floor above but I'd chosen to stay in Vanessa's. Once the local police had got over their unalloyed delight at having me in their midst, their first instinct was to give me an office and spend the rest of the inquiry tiptoeing past my door. The police believe they have enough problems without the weirdos from the KDA complicating things.

Most police – obviously Vanessa was different.

'Really? Which aspect do you find lacking?' I asked.

I was logged into the Rheinland-Pfälzer's LaPo computer and making random keyword searches of their crime database to see if anything relevant jumped out.

'The lack of focus for one,' she said. 'We drift from crime scene to autopsy to the victim's house and look for . . . I don't know what we're looking for. What are we looking for?'

'We're looking for the intangible,' I said. 'And the problem with the intangible is that it's pretty bloody hard to get your hands on.'

Try going into the prosecutor's office and saying that you know a suspect did it because of the vague sense of unease you had at the crime scene.

'Your colleagues are perfectly capable of following up the mundane leads,' I said. 'That leaves us with the things that aren't there.'

'But we still have special witnesses,' she said. 'Like your friend at the fountain.'

'You saw how useful that was,' I said.

'So how do we find the intangible?'

I looked up from the computer. Vanessa was looking at me with narrowed eyes – tapping her pen against her cheek. I wasn't used to that kind of attention from my liaisons – usually they're under orders to speed me on my way.

'How would you find something invisible?' I asked.

Vanessa nodded to herself, the pen tapped rapidly for a second or two and then stopped.

'By looking for the shape it makes in the world,' she said. 'Like footprints in the sand or branches bending back on their own.'

'Yeah,' I said, trying not to sound too impressed. 'By looking for the shape it makes.'

'So, what shape *does* it make?'

'That depends,' I said. And, when Vanessa gave me a stare, said, 'If it was easy then they wouldn't need us, would they?'

'Let's start at the beginning, then,' said Vanessa. 'You call these supernatural incidents "infractions", yes?'

'When they're serious enough to warrant our attention,' I said. 'We don't come out for every haunting or bowl of curdled milk.'

'So what causes an "infraction"?' asked Vanessa.

I explained that there can be many first-causes behind an infraction, but the main ones in the KDA's experience were either exposure to, or the triggering of, special equipment left over from the Nazi era, or exposure to a supernatural entity or natural force.

'Such as Kelly and the child?' asked Vanessa.

'Precisely,' I said. 'Location spirits, ghosts, revenants and the like. By the way, did you get the girl's name?'

'I asked, but she wouldn't say.'

There's also vampires and elves, but decades of misplaced romanticism mean that however carefully you explain the dangers to colleagues, nobody ever believes you.

The other category was much less common.

'Deliberate instigation of an infraction by a practitioner or practitioner-group,' I said, which led predictably to Vanessa's next question.

'What's a practitioner?'

'Somebody who practises modern magic.'

'Like you?'

'Like me,' I said. 'Although I'm properly trained in safe procedure.'

'So magic is dangerous?'

'To the practitioner as well as the general public,' I said.

Vanessa stopped tapping her pen and, putting it down, started methodically stretching her fingers. I wondered if she was suffering from rheumatism or RSI but it looked habitual rather than painful.

'Dangerous how?' she asked.

Dangerous in that one question leads to another, and that to the next, and suddenly you're standing in a dark and dripping forest with nothing but a flamethrower to keep you warm.

'You saw the body,' I said. 'Dangerous like that.'

'Is that why it's restricted?'

'As I told you, if they're not careful, a practitioner can injure themselves also. You can give yourself serious brain damage.'

Vanessa had one of those desks that could be raised to allow upright working. She raised it, did the strange finger exercise again and then started typing on her computer.

'If we assume that Ferdinand Tietz based his statue on the goddess of the river Kyll . . .' She stopped typing and stared at me. 'Then she would be hundreds of years old.'

'Possibly thousands,' I said.

Vanessa's brow wrinkled, then cleared. She shrugged and went back to work.

'Perhaps he based other statues on people of a supernatural inclination,' she said. 'So if we grab images of the statues' faces and manipulate them to make them look a bit more lifelike . . .'

'We might be able to get our witnesses to identify

them,' I said. 'Perhaps that's why the statue of Staphylos was defaced – to prevent an identification.'

'Precisely.'

I did a global search for criminal statue defacement in Trier and got nothing. But when I expanded it to all of Rheinland-Pfalz I found a reference as part of another case. A *Landgericht* Koblenz hearing in 1977 concerning one Heinrich Brandt, born 1945, who had attacked a statue at the Elector's castle in Molsberg but was deemed to be mentally incompetent. Six months earlier he'd been arrested at the French Officers' Casino for being drunk and disorderly, vandalism and trespass.

The damage was to the staircase and the statue of Methe.

'Not Staphylos?' Vanessa asked.

Brandt had claimed to have confused the statue with his wife.

'Although there was no record of him being married,' I said.

'Perhaps we should ask Kelly whether she knew him,' said Vanessa.

There were no further details on the computer, which wasn't unusual given that the crime had taken place twenty years before routine computerisation. Vanessa called the RLP archives, but they were closed for staff training that afternoon. There had been a couple of photocopies in the file dating from the late seventies. Heinrich Brandt had been briefly famous when a historian uncovered the circumstances of his birth. He'd been found orphaned, aged two weeks, in the rubble of his family home after the notorious RAF Christmas raids of 1944 pulverised Trier city centre. He was considered a Christmas miracle and was adopted by the Brandt family shortly after the end of the war. It was an unusual enough event that I considered calling the Research Department at the KDA, but it had just turned five and staff there would have all gone home.

Vanessa and I made a note to follow up first thing the next morning and called it a day.

*

After changing at the hotel I went for a jog down to the river path and ran south towards the hydroelectric power station. There and back again would be a little bit over eight kilometres – enough to stretch me out without making me tired.

I crossed the main road by the hospital and went down a steep flight of steps beside an old medieval crane with white walls and wooden cranes projecting from a witch's hat roof.

Being at least three metres below the level of the main road, the path was quiet and surprisingly deserted. I passed a couple of dog walkers and a knot of laughing children. Ahead I could see a pair of runners passing under the arch of the Roman bridge.

I love to run. Not just because it builds up stamina, and is always a useful skill for police, but because in the rhythm of my feet on the ground I find a space where I can think in peace. Or choose not to think at all, and lose myself in the physicality of the movement.

My mother, who keeps a copy of Sun Tzu by her bed, says that a wise person knows when to act and when not to act. My father agrees.

'Know when to speak,' he says. 'When to listen and, most importantly, when to call for backup.'

The sun had fallen behind the western ridge as I passed under the old stone arch of the Roman bridge. The valley was in shadow but the sky was a swathe of fading blue. Across the river the lights were coming on in the homes and hotels. There was no sign of the runners I'd seen earlier and, apart from the restless grumble of the main road, I could have been alone.

Only I wasn't.

I began to feel I was being followed.

Suspicion is a virtue in policing, and doubly so for magically trained police. Still, you've got to be pragmatic. As my father says, you must resist the temptation to become the job . . . or the job will destroy you.

I turned and jogged back for ten metres – there was nothing behind me.

I turned around again and ran on. Under the Konrad Adenauer Bridge with my footfalls echoing off the graffiti-covered concrete slabs. I listened carefully, but there was no echo, no second set of footsteps behind me.

And still I was sure I was being followed.

You can't go running in a shoulder holster. Not only do members of the public become alarmed at the sight of you, but a fully loaded pistol is heavy and throws off your balance. Since I'm forbidden to leave my service weapon in a hotel room safe, I'd taken the chance to leave it, and the dossier, safely locked in Vanessa's secure storage locker.

It grew darker, as if the shadows under the bridge had followed me down the footpath. There were trees growing along the riverbank and between them and the tree-covered elevation masking the road, it made it suddenly like running through a tunnel.

When the Newtonian synthesis came to Germany from England in the early eighteenth century its most famous centre was in Cologne, where the White Library took a proud but unobtrusive place somewhere between the university and the famous craft guilds of the city. The scholar practitioners of the White Library developed their own sophisticated and nuanced terminology to replace what the Director calls the maddening Anglo-Saxon vagueness of British wizardry.

While keeping the Latin names for the *formae* that are the building blocks of magic, they switched to the serious academic German of the time for everything else. Hence *Ortsgeist*: location spirit; *Schwebelicht*: palm-light; and *Seelen-Präsenz*: soul presence. Being methodical, they broke soul presence into sub-categories such as *Natur-Seelen-Präsenz*: natural soul presence; *Stadt-Seelen-Präsenz*: city soul presence; *Geister-Seelen-Präsenz*: spirit soul presence – which is what you feel when a ghost takes an interest in you – and *Ortsgeister-Seelen-Präsenz*: location spirit soul presence. It's extremely difficult to tell these various sensations apart and, as a result, German practitioners have spent the last three centuries cheerfully mislabelling everything around them.

The British, the Director sometimes concedes, might have had a point.

Still, there was no mistaking the sudden sensation of excited movement and chocolate-flavoured ice-cream for anything other than *Ortsgeister-Seelen-Präsenz*.

I was coming up on a set of steps that ran down to the water in one direction and up to the roadway in the other. Perfect for both a confrontation and a fast tactical retreat if things went wrong. There was also a gap in the trees that would allow me to see what was coming.

I stopped at the top of the steps and turned to face the river.

'Show yourself,' I said, and mentally rehearsed the shield spell the Director had drilled into me that spring.

The Mosel rolled past in the darkness. To my left was the impatient rumble of the barrage, behind me the swish of the evening's traffic.

Then I saw it. A pale streak in the water. The bow wave of something moving quickly just under the surface. It raced towards the steps and I took a deep breath to clear my mind.

The bow wave crested at the foot of the steps and flowed away to reveal a small figure in red-and-black-check pyjamas. It was the girl who'd been with Kelly in the square.

Her pyjamas were soaked and the water had straightened her ringlets so that they fell untidily to her shoulders.

'Hello,' I said in my best friendly manner, while not relaxing one bit.

The girl gave me an exasperated look. Then she shook herself, exactly like a dog, starting at her legs and working her way up to her crown and causing her hair to whip around her head. When she stopped she was completely dry.

'Come here,' she said, and her voice promised slides and swings and sunshine.

I felt the pull of her authority, but my first lesson from the Director had been how to resist the glamour.

It's exactly the same as resisting a bad habit – you just have to be aware of the problem and not let your unconscious talk you into anything you might regret the next morning.

Easier said than done – right?

'We can have fun.' She was as irresistible as a puppy.

'Why don't you come up here?' I said, keeping my tone light but implacable. It helps that my mother's a teacher of the unfailingly firm but fair variety. She's used that tone indiscriminately on my father and me since I can remember.

The girl tilted her head to one side for a moment and then skipped up the steps to join me on the path. Close up she smelt of turned soil, hayseed and peaches, with just a hint of motor oil behind it all.

I asked her name, and she said I could call her Morgane – her German was perfect.

'What do you want, Morgane?' I asked.

Morgane looked down at her bare feet and scuffed the ground with her toes.

'I want to see Vanessa again,' she said.

'Why are you telling me this?'

Morgane mumbled something inaudible.

'Pardon?'

'Kelly says I'm not to talk to her,' she said.

'Did she say why?'

'No.'

'Why do you think she doesn't want you to see Vanessa?'

Morgane looked up at me and squinted – her face was a pale oval in the twilight.

'Because she's a big meanie.'

'Or perhaps she's worried you'll be bad,' I said.

'I can be good,' said Morgane, hopping restlessly on one leg. 'I can be very good.'

'I believe you, but . . .'

'I can tell you something you don't know.'

Strangely, the intelligence on baby goddesses is a bit sparse. We've been getting unusual reports out of London for years, and hints from other countries. But this was the first time I'd had direct dealings with one. Making this, I was sure the Director would point out, an opportunity as well as a danger.

'Such as?'

'Stuff,' said Morgane. 'From before.'

'Before what?'

Morgane looked down to check that her feet were still attached to her legs and, satisfied they were, mumbled, 'Before I was here.'

'You remember that?'

'Sort of,' she said, but I recognised that tone from my own childhood as in: 'Have you done your homework?' 'Sort of . . .'

'Why don't you tell me what you know and I'll see what I can do about setting up a meet,' I said.

Morgane screwed up her face and then thrust out a small hand.

'Promise?' she said.

'I promise to try,' I said, and extended my hand.

Morgane harrumphed then shook my hand. Hers was warm and soft and for a moment my nostrils were filled with the scent of cherry blossom and I was bathed in the endless summer sun of my childhood.

Then the October chill crept in around the edges and the world darkened again.

'Do you know the Strackers that live up on the hill?' said Morgane, pointing downstream towards Ehrang. I said I did.

'Aunty Kelly had a boyfriend who she liked to kiss and kiss and kiss.' Morgane pulled a face at this inexplicable behaviour. 'Only he was like you, you know, going to die. And Aunty Kelly was sad and angry. So she did a bad thing to make him live longer. Only he died anyway and she was even more sad.'

'Do you know what she did?' I asked, but Morgane shook her head. 'Do you know when this happened?'

'A long long long long time ago,' she said. 'Now I've told you stuff. When can I go play with Vani?'

'I'll have to ask her first,' I said, which got me a long suspicious look. 'How can I contact you?'

'Easy,' she said. 'Put a note in a bottle and throw it in the river.'

'Can you read?'

'Of course I can read. French and German and' – she put a long stress on the second *and* – 'Luxembourgish.' She paused, waiting for praise.

'Very good,' I said. 'Aren't you clever?'

'Yes I am,' she said. 'And I have a very good memory as well.'

I just bet she did. It was going to be safest all round to at least ask Vanessa if she wanted to go out to play with Morgane.

We said goodbye and Morgane ran sure-footedly down the steps, jumped, wrapped her arms around her knees and, with a shriek of laughter, water-bombed the river.

The splash was unnaturally large and I had to jump back to avoid getting soaked.

To be on the safe side, I was going to have to teach Vanessa some basic resistance techniques. Which also meant I was going to have to inform the Director of what I was doing. I wasn't sure how she'd react.

And would the intelligence be worth it?

That's the thing about intelligence – you never know what it's worth until you test it.

I trotted up the steps, crossed the main road and ran back to my hotel on the Medardstraße, which was a nice safe hundred metres from the river.

6

Drinking Association

I was leaving the hotel breakfast room the next morning when Ziegler called me to say they'd located one of Jörg Koch's friends from the tattoo studio.

'The black one,' she said. 'We've asked him to come in for an interview this morning. Would you like to speak to him first?'

'Yes, please,' I said, and told her that I'd be down at the Post Office by eight.

'How are you finding Vanessa?' asked Ziegler – far too casually.

'She seems very efficient,' I said cautiously. 'Very enthusiastic.'

'Yes . . . enthusiastic,' said Ziegler slowly. And then, more normally, 'Good, good, glad to hear it.'

Vanessa was already in her office when I got in and collating the background on Kurt Omdale, who had been born in the Democratic Republic of Congo and had arrived in Hamburg with his parents in 1971. After school he had done an apprenticeship as a garage mechanic and was currently working as a supervisor at a garage on Bonner Straße on the West Bank. Less than a kilometre downriver from Jörg Koch's flat.

'How did they find him?' I asked.

'The hairdresser,' said Vanessa. 'Black people need special hair products.' Which was news to me.

'What kind of hair products?' I asked, but Vanessa didn't know.

'It was Ziegler's idea,' she said. 'She's married to an American pilot, a black guy. They have two daughters and she buys their hair products from that shop opposite the tattoo studio. She says there aren't that many places to buy such things in the city, so she checked to see if someone had popped in to make a purchase around the time Jörg Koch was getting his tattoo.'

Kurt Omdale hadn't bought anything. But he had entered to flirt with the shop assistant, who remembered because Kurt was a regular and he'd discussed tattoos.

'He said his friend was having a tattoo as a dare,' said Vanessa. 'He's asked to come in early so he can still attend church.'

Our conscientious Kurt was a large, good-looking black man with a square blunt face and tight curly hair that was greying at the temples. He was dressed in matching lightweight navy jacket and trousers, worn but well-maintained brown leather shoes and a pale blue pinstripe shirt which he wore open at the neck. His handshake, when we introduced ourselves, was firm and he took his seat confidently and without fear. Even after we'd read him his rights, which usually gives even the most upright citizen pause for thought.

'We've asked you here today in relation to the unfortunate death of Jörg Koch, with whom I believe you were acquainted,' said Vanessa.

You have to be careful with witnesses that you don't lead them into telling you things you want to hear. This desire to be 'helpful' can often be more frustrating than plain obstructionism.

'I can't believe Jörg is dead,' he said. 'I only saw him the other day.'

We knew that Ziegler had already informed him of the death and had asked preliminary questions. Vanessa and I both had his answers in our notes in front of us.

'When and where did you last see him?' asked Vanessa.

We'd purposely sat far enough apart so that Kurt had to turn his head to talk to us in turn.

'Last Saturday,' said Kurt. 'At our weekly meeting of . . . Well, we have a sort of club.'

'What kind of club?' I asked.

'I suppose you could call it a drinking club,' said Kurt. 'We call it the Good Wine Drinking Association.'

'And presumably you meet up and drink wine?' I said.

'Good wine,' said Kurt. 'It's an important distinction.'

'You drink good wine,' I said.

'That's how it started,' said Kurt. He hadn't been there when it started himself but the others had told him how it had been. Jörg Koch and Markus Nerlinger had met in a bar down the road from Jörg's flat. They'd both been regulars.

'They didn't know each other,' said Kurt. 'But one evening they just started talking.'

They found they had much in common. They were both on the wrong side of forty with little to show for it. Both were estranged from their families, Jörg by his divorce and Markus by his wife's death two years before.

'How did she die?' asked Vanessa.

'In hospital,' said Kurt. 'Cancer, I believe. So there

they were, gloomily drinking beer and comparing disappointments, when one of them quotes this bit of poetry: – *Life's too short to drink bad wine*. And the other says, "Then what are we drinking in this shithole for?"' I asked whether Kurt knew which of the two had said that, but he didn't know.

'Is it important?' he asked.

I shrugged. With the supernatural, first causes are often important.

Kurt said that the way it was told to him was that Jörg and Markus came to a decision simultaneously, stood up and, leaving their beers unfinished, left the bar never to return. They walked across the Roman bridge, up Karl-Marx-Straße and through the town centre until they found a bar that struck them as superior.

Kurt didn't know which one. The others had probably told him, but he didn't remember.

Inside they'd asked the waitress to recommend the best wine they had. This being Trier, the waitress had to ask her colleagues and there was a spirited discussion before a consensus emerged.

Kurt couldn't remember the name, only that it was a 2008 Riesling.

'Did they say whether it was a good wine?' I asked.

Kurt smiled.

'They said they had no idea of the absolute quality of the wine. Only that it was better than what they'd been drinking before. While they were refilling their glasses a man came to their table and introduced himself as Uwe Kinsmann. He apologised for interrupting but suggested that if they really wanted to appreciate the wine they needed to drink it slower.'

The men invited Uwe to join them and in return he bought the next bottle of wine. When they described what they were doing to Uwe, he asked to join their 'good wine club', which came as a surprise to Jörg and Markus because up to that point they hadn't known it existed.

'That's how the Good Wine Drinking Association was born,' said Kurt.

The three founder members quickly decided the rules. They would meet up every Saturday evening and drink good wine. Since they were in a city famous for its wineries it made sense that they'd pick a new one each week.

On their first official outing Markus brought Jonas Diekmeier, a younger man who worked in the office at Markus's factory. Despite being younger and quieter than the other members he fitted in perfectly.

'No family,' said Kurt. 'And the only people he was close to were on the internet. And living in the UK and America.'

'So how did *you* join?' asked Vanessa.

Kurt said he was coming to that.

Jörg had come in to Kurt's garage to pick up his car, but the work wasn't quite finished. Kurt, who'd been supervising that particular shift, had to apologise and offered coffee. They'd got chatting and by the time his car was ready Jörg had invited Kurt to the next meeting.

I asked what they'd talked about.

'The usual,' said Kurt. 'The economy, football, wine, women and man's futile quest for meaning in an uncaring materialistic universe.' We must have looked surprised because Kurt laughed. 'I took a course in philosophy at the People's College,' he said. 'But that came later.'

They met Simon Haas outside the winery and restaurant they'd chosen for their second official outing. He'd been staring at the menu for so long they'd taken pity on him and invited him to join.

And the drinking association might have stayed just that if on the next Saturday they hadn't forgotten to make a reservation.

'When we arrived the place was full,' said Kurt. 'It was the first warm evening of the year so we decided to buy some bottles and sandwiches and have a picnic by the river.'

'Whose idea was that?' I asked, but Kurt didn't remember.

'Anyway, before we got down to the old crane this good-looking girl and her friend came over with some leaflets and asked if we wanted to see a play,' said Kurt. 'They said they were trying to attract people who normally didn't go to the theatre, which I suppose was us, and would we like some free tickets.'

The Good Wine Drinking Association looked at each other and thought – why not?

They ended up back across the river in the European Academy of Fine Arts.

'You know,' said Kurt. 'That place opposite the big Kaufland supermarket.'

I looked at Vanessa, who nodded – she knew where he was talking about.

'What was the play?' I asked.

'I'm not sure,' said Kurt. 'Something by that famous English guy.'

'Shakespeare?' I asked.

'Oscar somebody,' said Kurt.

'Oscar Wilde?'

'That's the one,' said Kurt.

Bits of the play had been hilarious but Kurt admitted that a large part of the group's enjoyment was because all the parts were played by women.

'Young women,' said Kurt. 'Students.'

Afterwards they'd taken their wine and snacks and had their picnic in the dark and discussed the play and what to do next. Most of them couldn't remember the last time they'd been to the theatre.

'We don't do shit, do we?' Uwe Kinsmann had said. 'We're like birds that have forgotten how to fly.'

That's when they all agreed to expand the remit of the Good Wine Drinking Association beyond its original charter. They decided to come up with a list of new experiences that they could aspire to – the only restriction being that they couldn't be too expensive or interfere with work.

'What high cultural activity did you choose to do first?' asked Vanessa.

'We went to a strip club,' said Kurt. 'One of those on Karl-Marx-Straße.'

'Was it everything you imagined it was?' she asked. Kurt shrugged.

'It's nice to watch young women take their clothes off,' he said. 'But I thought it was a bit expensive.'

Kurt thought that they'd gone to an art exhibition at the university next, or it might have been their re-creation of gladiatorial combat up at the Roman circus. They used foam rubber weapons that Simon borrowed off a LARPer friend of his.

'LARP?' asked Vanessa.

'Live action role playing,' I said. 'Like role playing games with dice, only you wear costumes and act out the game.'

'It was tremendous fun,' said Kurt. 'I wouldn't have minded doing that again.'

And they'd done this in the Roman amphitheatre carved out of the ridge to the east of the city. If that wasn't a potential trigger event then I didn't know what was. I made a note to check the amphitheatre as soon as possible.

Kurt was hazy as to the order, but he was certain that they'd spent one Saturday collecting rubbish along the right-hand riverbank between the Roman and the Kaiser-Wilhelm bridges. One old man had assumed they were from the city and castigated them for never cleaning the area behind his block of flats. So the next day, a Sunday, they went and did his block of flats as well. Jörg, who was an electrician, fixed the porch light and intercom system while they were there.

After that, the Good Wine Drinking Association ceased to be just a Saturday thing and got more elaborate and time-consuming. Like the occasion they enrolled in random courses at the People's College.

'Uwe cut a list of evening courses into strips and put them in a bag,' said Kurt. 'And we each pulled out one at random.'

We asked who did what courses.

'I got philosophy for beginners, Markus got pottery, I think, Jörg got life drawing,' said Kurt, which explained the sketches we'd found in Jörg's flat. 'Simon did bakery, Jonas . . .' Kurt clicked his fingers a couple of times to spark his memory. 'Creative sewing. And Uwe did home brewing. That kept us busy until this summer, although we still met up for a drink and social events.'

'Such as?'

'My engagement party for one,' he said. 'I met my fiancée at the philosophy course and we went on cultural trips – mostly local. We went to Molsberg to see Simon's uncle.'

I saw Vanessa frown – Molsberg was where Heinrich Brandt, statue assailant, had got himself committed for a psychiatric evaluation.

'What did you do there?' asked Vanessa.

'Did some sightseeing and drank some wine of course,' he said.

'So what's to see in Molsberg?' I asked.

'Some old buildings, a castle with a beautiful garden.' Kurt shrugged. 'Simon's uncle ran one of those action-adventure camps for kids. We stayed over and helped out for sports day.'

A rueful expression crossed Kurt's face.

'Do either of you have children?' asked Kurt.

We made non-committal noises.

'I have three by my first marriage who must be grown up by now,' he said.

'You've lost touch?' asked Vanessa.

'They're in America with their mother,' he said. 'But as the wise man said, life's too short to drink bad wine. Regret is a terrible vintage.'

'And you have a fiancée?' said Vanessa.

Kurt said yes, and we gently prised her details out of him without seeming terribly obvious. After we'd established that, I cross-checked my notes and found we'd missed a question.

'You said you saw Jörg last Saturday, but you never said where.'

'A new place on Niederstraße,' said Kurt.

'Niederstraße in Ehrang?' said Vanessa.

'That's right,' said Kurt. 'Just past the church.'

It was a special event and they'd been lucky to get a reservation. A brand new winery, or rather an old one that had recently restarted production. Neither Vanessa nor I really needed to ask the name of the winery but we did anyway. That's good police work.

'Strackers,' said Kurt.

*

If you have access to land with the right terroir, anyone can plant vines and make wine. If you keep the number of vines below ninety-nine you don't even need a licence to do it. For those with a yen to make a living from the soil and fill in a van load of forms you needed at least eight hectares under cultivation to break even. Most wineries in the Mosel valley were half that size and stayed profitable by running a restaurant as well.

'Not only do you get a steady income from the restaurant proper,' said Vanessa, 'but you get to sell your wine at restaurant prices while creating goodwill and good publicity.'

Frau Stracker had twelve hectares under cultivation, but as a winery coming back from obscurity she needed a platform to relaunch her label. To this end she'd purchased a half share in the Restaurant Eifel, brought in an expensive English chef and spent heavily on promotion.

'She's looking to get a Michelin star,' said Vanessa.

'Do we know where all this money is coming from?' I asked.

Vanessa flicked through her papers.

'She owns a substantial share in a winery in California,' she said. 'We're still waiting on our request to the Federal Centre for Taxation.'

I'd told Vanessa about my evening talk with Morgane, although I'd left out the bit about her future play date. So it wasn't a surprise when she suggested that we bring Frau Stracker in for a chat.

'She may know more than she told us. She may even have been deliberately hiding something.'

'If so,' I said, 'why did she tell us about the wine sacrifice?'

Vanessa shrugged.

'She wouldn't be the first suspect to drop themselves in it,' she said.

'Let's check out the restaurant first,' I said. 'If the infraction started there then I might be able to pick up a trace.'

'You can do that?'

'If it's a noisy infraction, then yes,' I said. 'If it's subtle – perhaps not.'

'Still, the more we find out about Frau Stracker the better, I think,' said Vanessa.

'Can't argue with that,' I said.

*

The Restaurant Eifel took up the ground floor of a three-storey building with white walls and red-tiled roof. It was indeed just down from the church, which was an imposing edifice of reddish-brown stone that looked like someone had taken a normal parish church and stretched it upwards. I couldn't hear any singing, so either services were over or the congregation was struck dumb by the height of the ceiling. The rest of the street was just as quiet, and the restaurant's façade was shuttered. I checked my watch – it was just past ten o'clock.

'I think we're a bit early,' I said.

Vanessa peered in through the glass front doors.

'Somebody's in there,' she said. 'I can see a bag on a table and some keys.' She knocked a couple of times, but there was no reply.

While we were waiting I looked both ways down the street – trying to orientate myself.

'Have you noticed,' I said, 'that if you drew a straight line from our crime scene to where we left the wine sacrifice, this restaurant would be right on it?'

'Is that significant?' asked Vanessa as she banged on the door again – harder this time.

If you crossed the road you could follow the ridge as it rose behind the town and just see the beginnings of the Stracker vineyards.

'I don't know,' I said.

'Let's check around the back, then,' she said.

This part of Ehrang had been built on the old medieval pattern so that the individual buildings had a relatively narrow frontage, but extended back from the road much further than you might expect. This meant that there wasn't a back as such, but there was an alley leading to a courtyard. It was neatly kept but a couple of industrial-sized waste bins gave the space a fruity rotten smell. There was a back door that gave direct access to the kitchens, and we could have used that as an excuse to enter the premises without a warrant. If we hadn't just tripped over a body.

Because he was lying face down, it was impossible to say more than that it was an adult male dressed in jeans and a T-shirt.

I pulled my gun from its holster and stood watch while Vanessa checked his neck for a pulse. She shook her head.

'He's still warm,' she said. And, getting her phone out, called it in.

7

Special Circumstances

With a homicide the first job of the cops on the spot is to secure the crime scene and, if possible, check to make sure there are no witnesses and/or suspects trying to sneak off without fulfilling their civil obligation to help the police with their inquiries.

Just to be on the safe side, we did this with our pistols in our hands – although we kept them by our sides and our fingers out of our trigger guards. You don't want to shoot somebody's cat by accident.

Inside, the restaurant was dim and echoing. Daylight filtered in to gleam off varnished pine tables and the archaic brass fittings and hunting prints hung on the walls. The canvas shoulder bag and keys were where we'd seen them through the door. We didn't waste time checking the bag – better to leave that to the colleagues from K17. We cleared kitchen, stores, dining room and toilets as quickly as we could and went back to guard the corpse.

Vanessa timed how long it took Ziegler to arrive.

'Fifteen minutes on a Sunday,' she said. 'That's got to be a record.'

I stepped back and let them get on with it. I'd already done a survey for *vestigia* and found nothing. Although, as I told Vanessa, it didn't mean the crime wasn't super-natural.

'If it is a crime,' I said, since there were no obvious signs of foul play.

'I'm sure it's just a total coincidence,' said Vanessa.

Still, I didn't formally declare the case an infraction because the Director has drummed it into me that the KDA is not there for the local police to palm their work off on.

*

At least the victim was considerate enough to be carrying identification in his wallet. His name was Jason Agnelli, aged twenty-six, a British citizen and, presumably, the wonder chef brought in to put the Restaurant Eifel on the map.

'He's certainly going to do that,' said Vanessa.

We agreed with Ziegler that, since we already had a relationship, Vanessa and I would bring in Frau Stracker for an interview while Ziegler stepped up the hunt for the other members of the Good Wine Drinking Association.

'Do you think they're potential suspects?' asked Ziegler.

'I don't know,' I said.

'In that case,' she said, 'do you think that they're at risk?'

'Better safe than sorry,' I said. Which earned me a disgusted look from Ziegler.

Unfortunately Frau Stracker wasn't at her winery when we drove up, but one of the workers pointed us down a lane to the top of one of the vineyards. The one, we couldn't help noticing, that sloped down to the track where Jörg Koch's body had been found.

We encountered her climbing up the steep path and she seemed oddly pleased to see us.

'Thank God,' she said, 'I was wondering what to do next.'

She turned smartly about and led us down to the bottom of the vineyard. There was no grass here; instead the soil between the rows of vines was bare and covered with flat pieces of blue slate. You wouldn't want to slide down this hill on your back, I thought, you'd be cut to pieces.

We were halfway down when we saw the problem.

'That can't be good,' said Vanessa.

Modern vines are strung along metal wires suspended between metal or wood uprights. The green tops are cropped to ensure that the vine's energy budget – that's what Frau Stracker called it, the energy budget – goes into the fruit as much as possible. It also meant that it was easy to see the bunches of grapes – and the grey fuzz that laced them together like old cobwebs.

Even worse was the way the affected area radiated out in a rough semicircle from the bottom of the field. The centre was right at the point where Jörg Koch's body had been found. I could see the police tape marking the spot.

I asked Frau Stracker whether she'd touched anything with her bare hands. She looked alarmed and raised her right hand to stare at it, which answered that question. Vanessa dug out a small bottle of anti-bacterial hand gel and passed it over. I asked Frau Stracker when she'd last checked this particular field.

'Yesterday morning,' she said. 'There was no sign of infection then.'

So, at a rough estimate the fungus had covered a

hundred and fifty square metres in just over twenty-four hours.

As Frau Stracker washed her hands I had a closer look at the area of infection. It looked like the pictures of infected grapes that Vanessa had dug up on the internet. It also looked like the grapes held by the statue of Staphylos. Which meant, I was willing to bet, that the sculptor Ferdinand Tietz had seen such infected grapes in person. I pulled on my evidence gloves and the white filter mask I keep in my pocket for emergencies, and got as close as I could without touching an infected plant.

I caught the *vestigia* immediately, the same wriggling organic vitality I'd felt both at the crime scene and Jörg Koch's autopsy. Only now the violin sound felt more human, or at least more organic, like the wailing at a foreign funeral or some animal keening far away in the night.

The Director has always stressed the need to remain rational in the face of the inexplicable.

'You can't let fear drive you,' she says. 'But you can't let it paralyse you either. You must know when to take decisive action, even when it seems extreme, to prevent future harm.'

I stepped back, stripped off my gloves and, being careful not to touch their exterior, tossed them into the affected area. Then I called the Director and said that I needed her to authorise a sterilisation.

'What is it, and how large?' she asked.

In the background I could hear cheering and an excited commentary in Spanish. At a guess the Director had been settling in to watch football.

'A possible malignancy spread over two to three

hundred square metres,' I said, to allow for a safety margin. 'A large section of a vineyard.'

'How public?'

'People are going to see the smoke,' I said.

Somebody must have scored a goal because the roar of the crowd and the commentator having hysterics drowned out the sound of the Director swearing.

'All right,' she said finally. 'But I want you to stay on site and supervise. We don't want a repeat of what happened in Lüneburg – Deutsche Bahn still haven't forgiven us for that.'

You'd think those locomotives were made of solid gold the way they carried on.

'Understood.'

We finalised our plans to ruin everyone's Sunday and the Director went back to her football. I returned to Frau Stracker to give her the glad tidings, but before I could speak she asked me whether it was true Jason Agnelli was dead.

I looked over her shoulder at Vanessa, who mimed answering a phone to show it wasn't her fault.

'I'm afraid he was found dead this morning,' I said.

'How did he die?'

'We don't know,' I said.

'Is it related to the other death?' she asked, and then pointed at the infected area of her vineyard. 'Is it related to *that*?'

'We don't know,' I said. 'But just to be on the safe side we're going to incinerate half the field.'

Frau Stracker stared at me and her mouth formed the word *incinerate*. Then she looked first at the affected area and then back at me.

'Will there be compensation?'

'Yes,' I said. 'The rest of your crop won't be destroyed by an uncontrolled fungal infection.'

She looked back at the affected area, lips pursed.

'How can I help?' she said finally.

I asked if she had any machinery, such as a mini-digger, that could work on the sheer slope. But she shook her head.

'Far too steep. This is all worked by hand.'

'We're going to need a fire break around the burn area,' I said.

She nodded and said she could get her people to clear a break that morning. Sunday not being a day of rest in the wine industry – at least not during harvest.

'But afterwards you and I are going to have a conversation,' she said.

I said of course we would, but left out the fact that Frau Stracker's family history was now an official line of inquiry. I was sure I could slip that into the conversation at an appropriate time.

Vanessa watched Frau Stracker stride back up the slope and walked over to ask what next. I told her about the sterilisation, which she took with the same unnerving calm she had taken everything so far. I'd have asked the Research Department back at Meckenheim to dig into her family background for signs of ancestral connections to the supernatural if I wasn't pretty certain that the Director had already started that process.

'I have to stay here,' I said. 'So you'll have to go with the body to Mainz and supervise the autopsy.'

'But it's Sunday,' she said.

Unlike us poor foot soldiers on the front line, the

rest of the state apparatus of justice likes to work office hours. That usually included pathologists but not, I told Vanessa, Professor Doctor Carmela Weissbachmann.

'For her this will be Christmas morning,' I said. 'She won't want to wait.'

I briefed her on how to handle Carmela, and a couple of things to look for, and then watched as she puffed her way up the slope. Then I was alone with just the fungus for company. The slope was really so steep that one only had to lean back ten centimetres to sit down. I made myself comfortable, because when the Director says she wants you to supervise she means that she doesn't want you to take your eyes off the problem until the problem is solved.

'You can always pee in a bottle if you have to,' she says. Not that I had a bottle.

It was just past noon and the sky was full of scattered clouds sweeping their shadows up the valley. Beyond the lane at the bottom of the field, and the railway that ran alongside, the houses of Ehrang gave way to a patchwork of green and yellow fields that covered the flood plain to the hills in the distance.

Jörg Koch had died in a ditch in the lane below me, covered in *Botrytis cinerea* fungus and suffocated when it grew into his lungs. The fast growth and the suffocation both apparently impossible events. Or at least, impossible without a bit of supernatural help.

Magic could do such things, according to Dr Hugo Braun, whom the Director rates as the most reliable of the Weimar practitioners. In his *Wechselwirkungen zwischen der physischen und metaphysischen Sphäre* he wrote that 'Whatever the ultimate source of the power we call magic proves to be, it seems capable of interacting with the material world at the atomic level. Therefore it seems a trivial matter for this power to be deployed at the cellular level to accelerate or alter the fundamental nature of the organism.'

Reliable, perhaps. Easy to read? Not so much.

The older romantics of the White Library in Cologne had talked about the transformative power of magic and how it interacted with nature to create wonders. I looked at the white fungal infection that radiated out from the point where Jörg Koch had died.

Wonders indeed, I thought.

But even those misty-eyed lovers of the untrammelled mountain peaks recognised that magic could imbue nature with a hostile spirit, one that actively sought to kill, maim and destroy. When such things took the forms of animals or people they attracted names for each category – revenants, feasters, eye thieves. And everybody's Gothic favourite – the vampire.

When it's still – when it's the cellar of a house, or a ring of mushrooms in a forest or a gun emplacement outside Offenburg – it's called one of two things. If it remains static and unchanging then we call it *a despair*. If it seeks to extend its influence then it is *a malignancy*. Or as the Director puts it – a despair will suck you in, but a malignancy is coming to get you.

The death of Jörg Koch had triggered a malignancy. But why? We knew that the year before Herr Koch had teamed up with a bunch of other middle-aged male losers to accidentally form the Good Wine Drinking Association. I was willing to bet that this had led to the change in his life – the reconnection with his wife and kids. Kurt Omdale, fellow Good Wine imbiber, had also found new connections in the form of a fiancée. Had the other members of the association had similar transformations? And, if they had, were these improvements in their lives a natural or a supernatural phenomenon? And was that change related, directly or indirectly, with the malignancy that festered in the vineyard less than five metres from where I sat? I felt a chill that had nothing to with the weather.

I looked at the edge of the infection. Had the lacy white strands of fungus jumped to the next vine? I had the horrible sensation that it was growing right in front of my eyes, and I wished I'd thought to put down a marker to judge whether that was true.

Peter Grant would have put down a marker, I thought. *He probably would have used a laser rangefinder to measure the rate of growth in millimetres per hour.*

It occurred to me that while I knew everything the embassy and the BND in London could gather on *Detective Constable* Grant, he probably didn't know I existed. It was a comforting thought – I had enough problems in my life without letting the English get involved.

I counted vines from the edge of the malignancy to the next uncontaminated metal upright and made a mental note. If it was expanding rapidly I might have to improvise before help arrived. You can't use magic against something that feeds off magic, but you can use magic to slosh petrol over a wide area if you don't mind burning your eyebrows off.

Or causing a bit of collateral damage.

Morgane had said that Kelly, goddess of the river Kyll, had once tried to make a mortal lover, an ancestor of

Frau Stracker no less, immortal. But it had gone wrong. A *long, long long time ago*, she'd said. Had that been when Kelly was posing for Ferdinand Tietz as a model for Methe? Had the statue of Staphylos, Methe's husband, been modelled on Kelly's lover?

That was a series of shaky assumptions. But if we could interview Kelly again . . .

Had the statue been defaced out of rage, mischief, or to hide the lover's identity? Morgane had said that the lover had died. But there are people, and things that look like people, for whom death is just the beginning of a long career.

We needed to find a photograph of the statue of Staphylos with its face intact. That was a job for the Research Department back in Meckenheim.

We needed to trace the other members of the Good Wine Drinking Association and make a timeline of all their social events – most of which I could leave to the Trier police. Then we needed to assess whether any of those events had acted as a trigger to an infraction that had led to Jörg Koch's death and this malignancy – that would be my job.

Not forgetting the need to discover whether the tragic love affair between the ancestral Stracker and the laughing goddess of the river Kyll had any bearing on the case at all. Although my bet was that it did.

You can't pressure a river goddess unless you want to bankrupt your local flood insurance scheme. But Kelly was *in loco parentis* to Morgane, and Morgane wanted a play date with Vanessa.

I looked over at the malignancy and tried to judge whether it had spread down the row I'd mentally earmarked. I was sure it might have advanced a centi-metre or two. Perhaps, I thought, I can requisition a laser rangefinder after the job's done.

My phone pinged with a text with a caller ID of *Besondere Umstände*, telling me that they would arrive in approximately eighty minutes. The Special Circum-stances team were on their way. I sent them the location on Google Maps and asked them to pick up snacks on the way, and received a thumbs up emoji by way of reply. Then I went down the slope to where a stand of vines screened me from both the road and anyone up on the ridge above, and had a piss.

*

Besondere Umstände – Special Circumstances, also known as the fire brigade and/or reality control – is the KDA's rapid response team. In the fifties and sixties there were half a dozen teams based around the country and each had its own armoured personnel carriers and helicopters. As all the main werewolf caches and 'sites of historical interest' were cleared and neutralised, their numbers shrank. And despite a brief surge of activity following reunification, they were down to one team based in a small industrial park outside Wiesbaden.

They'd also lost the helicopters and the army surplus armour, but gained a fleet of nondescript Mercedes Sprinter vans that caused a great deal less comment. Likewise, they dropped their forest-green uniform in 2003 and instead turn out in jeans, corduroys and, iron-ically, army surplus jackets. Which made them almost indistinguishable from Frau Stracker's workers, who were currently clearing the firebreak at the top of the field. These days when Special Circumstances roll into town, people start asking what band they roadie for.

Earth, Wind & Fire, I thought, as I saw the first of the Mercedes park on the lane below. Which, strangely, was the band I reckon was the one thing my parents must have had in common all those years ago, because it sure as hell wasn't the role of nuclear energy in the economic development of the nation.

Special Circumstances were led by Elton Schuster, a former captain in the pioneers, an irrepressible man in his late thirties who had embraced his new role with huge enthusiasm. Not least because it allowed him to blow things up as well as fix them. He came bounding up the field towards me, radio in one hand and a wooden walking stick in the other.

'Tobi,' he called, 'you never disappoint me.'

I introduced him to Frau Stracker and watched while they tried to out-rural each other. Elton is from a small village in eastern Saxony, so naturally he won, although it was surprisingly close. He inspected the firebreak and declared it suitable.

'But let's try to avoid needing it,' he said.

I stayed where I was sitting and let them get on with it.

In the meantime one of Elton's minions, a young blonde woman in a Russian-pattern camouflage jacket three sizes too large for her, dropped a plastic bag in my lap. Inside were a couple of bottles of apple spritzer and a slightly dented chicken schnitzel sandwich wrapped in greaseproof paper.

Frau Stracker sat down next to me and I gave her one of the bottles of apple spritzer.

Trier, I thought, is not so large a town that people don't know each other.

'Does the name Heinrich Brandt mean anything to you?' I asked, because it's always worth a try.

'Not a happy memory,' said Frau Stracker.

'Why's that?'

'He tried to rape me when I was twelve,' she said.

8

Service Weapon

Listen.

That's how I'm trained to deal with revelations like that.

Listen. Do not push, not even gently. If somebody mentions a secret, and I knew this was a secret because there was no record of a sexual assault in Frau Stracker's files, then it means they probably want to talk about it. To someone. You're probably not their first choice, but you're a stranger and sympathetic and detached.

All you have to do is make it clear that you're listening, that you're paying attention and that you're not going to make any judgements.

True, my training centres around getting victims of supernatural trauma to give coherent statements. But the principle is the same.

We sat in silence for a while watching Elton directing his people. They were mounting what looked like large paint cans with spikes welded to their bases at regular intervals around the malignancy.

'It's a little bit like a vapour cloud explosion,' he'd said when I'd asked him what he planned. 'Only slower, less explosive and more controlled. We don't want to flatten the neighbourhood after all, do we?'

'Do we need to move back?'

Elton had squinted at the lie of the land.

'No,' he'd said. 'You should be fine where you are.'

I decided I was going to move back when the time came.

'I think he was a friend of my father's,' said Frau Stracker. 'I didn't notice him much, he was a grown-up and I was a girl. You don't pay much attention to your parents' friends, do you? Unless they're famous or glamorous or something like that. Do you?'

I paused to indicate that I was giving it some thought.

'No,' I said. 'You don't, do you?'

'My father was a lawyer, my mother was a housewife, my older sister took after my father,' said Frau Stracker. 'She works in Düsseldorf now. Grandfather was the only one interested in the winery and I was the only one interested in hanging around with Grandfather.'

'Did your parents mind?'

'I think they believed it would keep both of us out of mischief,' she said and smiled.

'Did it?'

'Not noticeably,' she said. 'He was a terrible old man in some ways.'

Downslope, Elton raised his voice.

'Be careful!' he shouted. And then, in response to a reply we couldn't hear, 'Yes, the detonators are stable. But the accelerant is sticky, doesn't wash off with water and is inflammable. I don't want any of you spontaneously combusting on the trip home.' A pause. 'Again!'

'Up until then I don't think anything really bad had ever happened to me,' said Frau Stracker. 'I ran into

Heinrich, actually, down there.' She pointed to the lane at the bottom of the steeply sloped field.

'Just there?' I asked, indicating where Jörg Koch's body had been found.

'No, further that way.' She pointed south – towards where the lane joined the Niederstraße and the houses began. 'I'd been to the shops and I was coming back. There's a track up through the woods that goes all the way to the winery just short of this vineyard.'

Heinrich Brandt had appeared as if from nowhere and called her name. He'd had to remind Frau Stracker who he was.

'He said, "Hello, Jacky. Are you going to see your grandfather?"' Frau Stracker shook her head. 'Only my father called me Jacky and he said he knew him from work.'

When she said she was, he offered her a lift. She said no, and that it was quicker to go up via the footpath.

I didn't want to break Frau Stracker's flow, but I did think it was telling that she didn't accept the lift. Caution, perhaps. Or had she subconsciously noted something odd?

In that case, Heinrich said, he would accompany her up the path. So as Jacky skipped along it, Heinrich laboured after her. It was a hot day and trees left a resin scent in the still air. Every thirty metres or so Heinrich would call out to Jacky to slow down and she would stop to let him catch up. When they came out of the woods at the top of the slope they paused to look back over the valley.

'He said he could see his house. And he was totally normal, like any other grown-up,' said Frau Stracker.

The change came as they walked along the lane from the edge of the woods to the winery, the same compound Vanessa and I had visited that first evening. Her grandfather didn't live there. He had a house further up the ridge in Pflanzgarten, but he was reliably at the winery at that time of year.

Jacky didn't notice the change at first. Heinrich had been talking to her about how pretty she was, and asking what she wanted to do when she grew up, and Jacky had mostly tuned him out. Right up until he put his hand on her shoulder.

'Like he was my father,' she said.

Jacky tried to twist out of his grasp, but his grip grew stronger. Enough, she found later, to leave bruises. Heinrich told Jacky that he loved her.

'He said it very seriously,' said Frau Stracker. 'As if I was a grown woman with whom he was having a relationship – a proper grown-up relationship.'

Not that Jacky had caught that nuance, or would have cared if she had.

'I had that strange disconnect like when a friendly dog growls and bares its teeth at you. You can't believe it's the same dog,' she said. 'He called me "my love", "my beauty", "my precious one".'

Jacky bit his arm until he let go – hard enough to draw blood – and ran for her life.

She was young, healthy and light on her feet, but every time she risked a look over her shoulder Heinrich was right behind her. She'd been hoping that her grandfather, or at least somebody, would be at the winery. But as she ran into the compound nobody was around. She sprinted for the door to the cellar yelling for her grandfather, but nobody came. In her mind Heinrich was right behind her, hands reaching for her back. But when she turned at the door to check, she found he'd stopped in the middle of the compound next to one of the old trailers.

When he saw Jacky looking, he shook his head sadly.

'It's destiny,' he said. 'There's no escape for you or me.'

Jacky slammed the door and bolted it.

It was a good solid door and she had faith in it.

'There was no phone in the cellar in those days,' said Frau Stracker. 'Or Wi-Fi.'

She knew that she just had to sit tight until her grandfather returned.

But then Heinrich started to smash the door down.

'He must have found a sledgehammer or some other heavy tool,' said Frau Stracker. 'I heard him grunt, like an animal, and there was this crash and the whole door shook.'

There had been a second blow which splintered the planks, and a third that smashed a hole clear through the door.

'I was so scared that I wet my pants,' said Frau Stracker. 'But I knew something he didn't.'

'What was that?' I asked.

'Grandfather kept his pistol in the desk drawer,' she said.

It was a Walther P38, a souvenir her grandfather had acquired during the war despite never having served beyond a couple of months in the *Volkssturm* towards the end. He'd used it to shoot at deer and wild pigs when they trespassed on the vineyards. Less trouble than a rifle, he'd said, when all you wanted to do was scare things off.

'He'd shown me how to fire it,' said Frau Stracker.

No wonder he was your favourite, I thought.

Jacky had retreated to the far end of the cellar with the gun and waited. When the door failed and Heinrich crashed down the stairs, she raised the pistol in the proper two-handed grip her grandfather had taught her and aimed at the spot she thought he'd be when he reached the bottom of the steps.

'I had some notion,' said Frau Stracker, 'that I would warn him first. But as soon as I saw him I fired.'

As many times as she could. More than twice, probably less than six. The noise of the gun was so loud that the pain in her ears made her close her eyes. And, when she opened them again, Heinrich was gone.

'Did you hit him?' I had to ask.

'I don't know,' said Frau Stracker. 'But Grandfather found blood on the steps.'

Jacky's grandfather had returned to find her washing her shorts and undies in the sink at the back of the cellar. What with the blood and the lingering smell of gunfire, it didn't take him long to tease the story out of Jacky.

He reloaded the pistol, fetched one of the women who worked for him to take Jacky home and went to see if he could find Heinrich Brandt. I noticed that at no point did 'calling the police' seem to have been an option.

'It was strange,' said Frau Stracker. 'I went home, had a bath, changed my clothes and when my parents came home I sat down and had supper. When they asked what I'd done all day I said I'd helped prune the vines and had a big late lunch with Grandpapa and the workers, which was why I wasn't that hungry.'

She went back to see her grandfather the next day.

'Only I didn't use the path through the woods,' said Frau Stracker. 'I came up this path here.' She indicated the path we sat on. 'I wasn't afraid at all – isn't that strange? I've always felt safe around these fields. But I've never gone through the woods again – not even now.'

Her grandfather sat her down with a glass of wine and asked if she was all right. He explained that he hadn't been able to find Heinrich, but he'd alerted an old friend of his who was high up in the police and they were looking for him, too.

'But what if the police find out I shot him?' asked Jacky.

Grandfather showed her the bullet holes in the walls of the cellar and explained that he believed that none of her shots had struck home.

'You scared him off,' said her grandfather. 'Like one of those pigs, yes?'

It was plausible. I've fired a P38 a couple of times and they're heavy, industrial pistols which kick up and to the right. Even with a good two-handed grip an inexperienced twelve-year-old could easily miss with every shot.

I thought of the deformed lead pellet I'd found at the bottom of the field where Koch had been discovered and from where the malignancy had sprung. I'd have to call Wiesbaden and see if ballistics had identified it as a bullet. And if so, what calibre?

Had Heinrich Brandt staggered down the hill and died at that spot? If so, what had happened to the body?

Still, I didn't even know the lead pellet was a bullet,

yet let alone a 9mm round suitable for a P38. Jacky's grandfather might have been right. Jacky could have missed every shot.

I did plan to visit the cellar later and count the holes for myself, however.

Jacky wasn't too reassured by her grandfather's theories at first, but as days and then weeks went by without Heinrich reappearing she began to think she might be safe. When she dared ask her father, as casually as she could, what had happened to his friend Heinrich, she learnt that his disappearance was a mystery. And in any case, he hadn't really been a friend, more of an acquaintance.

'Grandfather said he was gone for good,' said Frau Stracker.

The way she said 'gone for good' set off police bells in my head.

'You think your grandfather did something to Heinrich Brandt, don't you?' I asked.

Frau Stracker shrugged.

'You think he killed him?' I asked, and she nodded slowly.

In which case we'd never find the body. Farmers make the best murderers because they have totally legitimate access to everything from plastic sheeting to industrial strength chemicals and heavy digging equipment. And, of course, stretches of land out of the prying eyes of strangers.

'I never saw the gun again,' she said. And then, after a long pause, 'Am I in trouble?'

No gun, no body, no witness, no grandfather?

'No,' I said. 'But I will need you to come down to the police station and make a formal statement.'

Frau Stracker said something but it didn't register because I realised that the vineyard in front of us had just been cleared of personnel. I was about to suggest that we move back up the slope when Elton dropped down beside us with a detonator in his hand.

'Ready?' he said, and before I could say anything gave the switch on the detonator a sharp twist.

Nothing happened.

'Wait for it,' said Elton. 'We have to get the right degree of saturation.'

It started at the bottom of the vineyard. A line of yellow and orange flame that rolled up the slope. Behind it boiled a wall of white smoke, shot through with black, that rose into the sky like a curtain flapping in the wind. The flames and smoke came charging up the slope towards us with a sound like cloth being ripped in two, and the heat struck the exposed skin of my face and hands and caused me to flinch backwards.

And then it was gone – quickly fading down to a smouldering line at the edge of the firebreak.

There were hollers and cheers from members of Special Circumstances and those of Frau Stracker's workers who'd stuck around to see the show.

'Damn,' said Elton as he surveyed his blackened handiwork.

'What?' I asked, suddenly alarmed again.

'We should have buried some potatoes along the edge,' he said. 'We could have had a feast.'

'You wouldn't make that joke if you'd seen the body,' I said.

'This is why I leave that part of the job to you,' he said.

9

High Places

Vanessa didn't get back from Mainz until late in the evening, but she gave me a preliminary report over the phone as she was driving home.

'He choked to death on his own vomit,' she said. 'He had a blood alcohol content of just over three per thousand.' Which was pretty much blind drunk, but not necessarily enough to kill you.

'That was a bit early in the morning,' I said. 'Even for an English guy.'

'Carmela thinks he was much drunker on Saturday night, passed out and choked about three in the morning,' said Vanessa. 'Give or take an hour or so.'

Carmela – and I noticed it was Carmela now, not Professor Doktor Weissbachmann – hadn't found any evidence of foul play, but Jason Agnelli's stomach had been noticeably distended and its content had been unusual.

'Partially macerated grapes in advanced state of fermentation,' said Vanessa. 'At least a litre's worth. They're going to run tests, but it's possible that the mash was the source of the alcohol.'

'He must have been really desperate for a drink,' I said.

'Pre-crushing the grapes is part of the winemaking process,' said Vanessa. 'Could this be a progression, first the infection, the pre-crushing . . . Could someone be following the winemaking process? Like a ritual or something?'

'That's an unpleasant thought,' I said. 'What would be next?'

'The pressing and then the fermentation proper,' she said.

You can't magic a litre of grape mash into someone's stomach, at least not without making the sort of hole that Carmela was bound to notice. But sometimes the simplest cruelties work the best.

'Was there any sign of coercion?' I asked.

'No cuts or bruises, no finger or ligature marks. Definitely no bruising or damage to the lips, soft palate or throat,' she said. 'Carmela said that the process looked entirely voluntary.' There was a pause while I heard Vanessa pull up at a crossing, indicate and pull out. 'I've seen drunks do some crazy things,' she said. 'But drinking a litre of fermented grapes?'

Somebody at K11 would be reaching out to the British police to see whether Jason Agnelli had a background of alcohol abuse or mental illness. I wished we could also reach out to our counterparts at the Folly, but we've yet to get ministerial permission to initiate a contact.

'Could it have been Kelly?' asked Vanessa, no doubt remembering how easily the location spirit had closed her mouth against her will. 'Could *you* make someone do that? Using . . . magic?'

'Not me, but a sufficiently trained practitioner could.'

That the Director could, I knew, because part of my

training had involved her using the technique on me until I built up a resistance. But such an assault would have involved an intensive spell, which would have left a trace.

'Did they recover a mobile phone?' I asked.

'It was sent to the lab,' she said. 'But they won't be open at this time.'

I suggested that she might as well go straight home and we could have an early start the next morning. Judging from the tone of her reply it had never occurred to her that we were going to do anything else. Before she hung up she did ask why the mobile phone was important.

'It might tell us what we're dealing with,' I said.

*

I got in to the Post Office at seven, having paused in the hotel breakfast room just long enough to fill a plastic bag with bread rolls, croissants and those tiny cinnamon rolls which you only get in three-star hotels. Unfortunately Ziegler was at the station even earlier and wanted a meeting which, because she was a *Polizeihauptkommissarin* and Vanessa and I were lowly *Kriminalkommissare*, meant we had to haul ourselves up two storeys to her office.

She told us that they'd traced the remaining members of the Good Wine Drinking Association and asked if I wanted to interview them first or would I prefer for K11 to get on with it.

'Given we've already had two deaths,' I said, 'we should contact them as soon as possible and bring them here for an interview. We need to establish a basic timeline for the crucial association meetings and alibis for two deaths.'

Ziegler tapped a fingernail on her desk. She also had one of those fancy desks, I noticed, that had an electric motor to raise or lower it so she could work standing up. Although why anyone would want to do desk work standing up has yet to be adequately explained to me.

'And what happens if one of them is a practitioner?' she asked, proving that she'd taken the time to ask her contacts about the KDA and what it does. 'Won't that be dangerous?'

I was about to say *not really*, but I remembered Vanessa's notion that perhaps Jason Agnelli had been magically compelled to drink the fermented grapes against his will. As a result of that thought, I spent the next hour writing a safety protocol for interviewing potential practitioners. This involved interviewing in pairs, and ensuring that one colleague is always placed behind the subject and has fast access to a CO_2 fire extinguisher.

'A fire extinguisher?' asked Vanessa.

'For distraction,' I said. 'It's hard to cast a spell when somebody sprays one at your head. A bucket of iced water is even better, but they tend to be a bit conspicuous in the normal policing environment.'

While I'd been occupied with that, Vanessa had waded through the two boxes of material that constituted the 1982 investigation into the disappearance of Heinrich Brandt. Occasionally she muttered to herself and made a note.

'You can tell they definitely knew about the attempted rape and the shooting,' she said after a while. 'But the lead investigator had obviously been told to leave it out of the report.'

'Frau Stracker did say her grandfather had a friend high up in the police,' I said.

'Judging by the careful absences in these reports that friend was *Polizeidirektor* or above,' said Vanessa and went back to her reading.

We were approaching the stage when one of us would have to go for a second coffee run when Vanessa said she had found something.

'The investigators thought Heinrich Brandt might have obtained a second car,' she said.

The car officially registered to his name and address, a brand new VW Polo, was found parked on the Niederstraße just short of where it was crossed by the railway bridge.

'It's obvious that they think Brandt waited in his car that morning for Jacky to walk past, but of course they can't say that because they're not supposed to know about the attack,' she said.

They'd searched the car and Heinrich's residence in the south of the city and found no indication that he had returned there after the attack. But early on the first morning after the attack on Jacky, a patrol had been sent to investigate a burnt-out vehicle on the Markusberg. This was another Polo, only an older model that had been deliberately set on fire – although the fire investigation officer claimed that they couldn't find any trace of an accelerant.

It's not that hard to set a car on fire – you can do it with a lighter and a strategically placed firelighter – but the expert was adamant the seat of the fire had been in the driving seat and that it looked like a Molotov cocktail had been thrown in the front. Only without the cocktail.

If I'd been there in 1982 this would have raised a definite alarm. But back then my parents were still arguing about deployment of intermediate range nuclear weapons or maybe getting down at the local discotheque – or possibly both at the same time.

The security services were briefly involved in case it was terrorist related, but quickly lost interest. As would the officers investigating the Heinrich Brandt case, if a bloodied shirt hadn't been found close by the burnt-out car. This led the investigators to trace the car's serial number, through the manufacturer and ultimately to the car's current owner, who had reported it stolen the afternoon of the shooting.

'From Quinter Straße,' she said. 'Which is in Quint.'

Which was the built-up area to the east of the Stracker winery – across the railway tracks.

Neither of us could work out why the investigators connected the shirt and this particular car, until we found the top page of a forensic report that had been misfiled in the wrong folder. There was no sign of the rest of the report.

'This file has been sanitised,' said Vanessa.

'Looks like it.'

From what we had, we were able to determine that it had been a man's blue, pinstriped shirt with extensive bloodstains. And bullet holes.

I'd already called Wiesbaden, who'd confirmed that the lead pellet was indeed a 9mm round but whether it had been fired from Grandfather's P38 was impossible to determine without the pistol. I'd also asked Elton and his Special Circumstances crew to dig up that section of the vineyard on the off chance Heinrich was buried under it, but they'd found nothing.

'Okay,' I said. 'Heinrich Brandt, having been shot and wounded somewhere in the torso, somehow staggers out of the basement, down the hill, across the railway tracks, steals a car. Drives it somewhere else, dumps it, sets it on fire . . .'

'Possibly using magic,' said Vanessa, jumping, I thought, to conclusions.

'Possibly,' I said. 'Not everything that's unexplained is caused by magic. Then he strips off his shirt and vanishes – again.'

'Again.'

'And this happened on the Markusberg?'

'At the Mariensäule.'

'Which is where?'

Vanessa led me over to the office window and pointed.

'Over there,' she said. 'At the top of the ridge.'

Across the river the ground rose steeply enough to shake off any buildings and revert to forest. At the top was a slender tower topped with a statue of the Virgin Mary. A horrible suspicion came over me – that if I'd just taken a moment to notice the thing when I drove into town on the first day, I might have saved myself a tremendous amount of time and effort.

'I think we should go and have a look,' I said. 'But first we're going to need a bottle.'

'What for?' asked Vanessa.

'Because we need to talk to Kelly again. And to do that we need to set you up with a play date with our irrepressible little river spirit.'

'Why me?' asked Vanessa, who was learning to be commendably suspicious.

'Because she likes you,' I said.

In the end we couldn't find a glass bottle, so we had to use an empty plastic Fanta bottle instead. I left the location of the play date to Vanessa, although I cautioned her to avoid sites too close to the river. Once that was decided, Vanessa wrote an invitation on some pink notepaper she found at the bottom of one of her desk drawers. We specified a time that afternoon.

'Do you think she'll turn up?' asked Vanessa.

'Morgane seemed very keen. I'm just hoping that Kelly is feeling protective enough to turn up as well,' I said.

*

We took Vanessa's vehicle, which turned out to be a brand new Dacia Duster, and stopped off on the Roman bridge to throw our message in a bottle into the river – but only after we checked that nobody from the council was watching.

After the defeat of Napoleon, Trier – along with the rest of the Rheinland – was handed over to the Kingdom of Prussia, as a reward for Blücher saving Wellington's arse at Waterloo. Being ruled over by a bunch of land-obsessed Protestant aristocrats was bound to cause tension. Resistance to rule-by-Junker manifested itself in a number of ways, not least by building a monument to the Virgin Mary three hundred metres up a sandstone ridge so that it overlooked the whole city.

There was nothing about it in the dossier, but Catholic monuments, especially in the West, were often over-looked by the *Ahnenerbe*.

'Why do you think it's so significant?' asked Vanessa, as the Dacia laboured up an insanely steep lane through the woods.

'It has to do with the way magic works,' I said.

'And how does it work?'

I don't normally explain the details of magic to colleagues outside the KDA. Apart from anything else, it always sounds so absurd when you say it out loud.

'We don't actually know what magic is,' I said as we reached the top of the ridge and entered the eerily quiet village of Markusberg. 'But we do know some of the things it does. It's like Isaac Newton and gravity.' This was the analogy the Director used when she was explaining it to me. 'Newton didn't need to know how gravity functions in order to work out that big masses attract each other over distance.'

'Well, if you knew how it worked it wouldn't be magic, would it?' said Vanessa.

I squirrelled that one away to impress the Director with later.

Beyond the village the road ran below the brow of the ridge into cool forest shadows and five hundred metres along there was a forlorn little bus stop, a parking area and steps leading up to the monument.

'This is where the burnt-out car was found,' said Vanessa.

We parked and walked up through the trees. I explained magic was generated by the environment, but it tended to build up around what the Director calls *Markante Orte*: distinctive places or prominences. Places or objects that stand out. In nature this can be old trees or rivers or rock formations.

'But where it really seems to accumulate,' I said, as we got to the top of the steps, 'is around man-made structures, the older the better. Castles, churches, old houses and, of course, great big ornamental columns on the tops of hills.'

The case in point – forty metres of neo-Gothic sandstone with the Virgin Mary at the top adorned with a halo of small stone spheres. Not that we could see the spheres from our lowly position at the base, but presumably God would be pleased with this view.

The column had originally been a pinkish brown, but the years had pocked and weathered it into a grey-green with patches of lichen mottling the lower sections in an interesting pattern. Graffiti was etched into the stone up to shoulder height. There was an iron door which led, Vanessa explained, to a staircase up to a viewing gallery. But it had been closed for over a hundred years.

'People used to throw themselves off the top,' she said.

'Isn't that a bit theologically unsound?'

'It would be a lovely view on the way down.'

'I'm going to check for residual magic,' I said.

'How do you do that, exactly?' asked Vanessa.

This is something I'm actually encouraged to teach to appropriate non-KDA colleagues. The rationale being that the more police who can tell a real infraction from random vandalism, animal cruelty or student pranks, the fewer wasted trips valuable KDA assets have to make. Since I am usually that valuable asset, I heartily approve of this approach.

I told her to stand close to the wall, put her palm against it and close her eyes.

'Try not to think about anything specific,' I said. 'Let your mind float freely.'

I expected her to say something clever. I did, the first time the Director told me to empty my mind. But Vanessa stood very still, her breathing slow and even.

I put my own hand on the wall.

'You know when you're lying in your bed on the edge of sleep?' I said. 'And you see random images and hear sounds?'

'Like daydreams,' she said.

The best practitioners, the Director once told me, are those that can dream with their eyes open.

'Yes,' I said. 'But don't try and influence it.'

'Right.'

I put my own hand on the rough sandstone of the column and asked Vanessa what she could see or feel. There was a slight breeze on my face and the rustle of leaves all around, the smell of damp grass and a faint whiff of urine where someone or some dog had decided that the monument was too good a lamppost to pass up.

I let it all drop away,

'I can smell smoke,' said Vanessa. 'And weird triangular patterns – like a kaleidoscope.'

Neither were coming through to me.

'Anything else?'

Vanessa's voice took on a strangely distant tone. 'Despair,' she said. 'Terrible despair.'

That was definitely there. A suicide – or possibly the aggregate of many suicides – the sudden deaths cementing the emotion into the stones.

'That's *vestigia*,' I said. 'Try and fix in your mind how that sensation differs from the earlier ones.'

'This is difficult,' she said.

'If it was easy,' I said, 'everybody would be doing it. Now what else?'

I could feel something underneath the despair, a now-familiar squirming unclean sensation like the feel of maggots wriggling across my skin.

'Somebody's watching us,' said Vanessa.

'No, that's not it,' I said.

'No,' said Vanessa. 'We're being watched from the trees to our left. Young man, wearing a cap and a blue padded jacket.'

'How long has he been there?'

'A couple of minutes,' said Vanessa. 'Shit – he's seen me looking.'

'We might as well introduce ourselves, then,' I said.

We peeled off the column and I saw him. A pale face broken by a screen of green leaves, a worried expression under a black baseball cap, a padded jacket, skinny jeans and trainers. A teenager, I thought, although old enough to have finished school.

'Hello, can you help me?' I said, and he turned and bolted down the footpath running north from the Mariensäule.

'Get the car,' I shouted to Vanessa and took off after him.

The young man ran with a beautifully relaxed gait and was so light-footed that he barely disturbed the leaves that covered the path. He was also, I couldn't help noticing, pulling quickly away.

I conjured a tangle-foot and threw it at his legs. But I'd left it too late – the spell only has an effective range of five metres at most, and the young man had a lead of ten metres now. I swore and dug in, but I was wearing my street shoes and they kept slipping on the leaves and soil.

On my left the ground fell away in an almost vertical drop towards the city and the river. To the right, a steep wooded slope ran down to the road. I heard an engine start up and risked a look to see if I could spot Vanessa in the car.

Fatal mistake – my left toe hit something under the leaves and I spent the next five or six strides flailing my arms to stay upright. By the time I'd regained my balance the young man had opened up his lead by a further couple of metres. I really would have been better off in bare feet.

Then he made his own mistake, turning to see whether I was still behind him. I stopped and bent over with my hands on my knees. He stood, staring back at me, his eyes wide as he fidgeted from foot to foot.

I didn't need to feign being out of breath, but I exaggerated my gasping to put him at his ease. I heard what I hoped was Vanessa's Duster pass by on the right – I couldn't look to confirm without tipping Running Boy off.

Once I estimated that Vanessa was far enough ahead, I straightened and gave him a cheery wave.

'I just want to talk,' I said.

And he was off again.

He got about ten metres before Vanessa stepped out from behind a tree, caught his arm and spun him around so that his own momentum landed him on his back. He held his hands up as if fearing an attack, but Vanessa simply grabbed his right arm and flipped him over on his front. Then she grabbed his other wrist and brought it behind his back as well, although she held off handcuffing him.

When I finally jogged up to them, we took an arm each and lifted the young man to his feet. I could feel him trembling under my hand and he was breathing hard. I also noticed that his cap had stayed firmly on his head despite his tumble. I looked closer – it was fastened much tighter than could be comfortable.

'Take off the hat,' I said.

'No, no, no,' he shouted, and would have backed away if Vanessa and I hadn't had a firm grip on an arm apiece.

'Sshhhh,' I said. 'Calm down. We're all *special* here.'

The young man hesitated at my emphasis on 'special' and looked wildly from my face to Vanessa's before his shoulders slumped and the tension drained away. I relaxed my grip enough to allow him to remove his cap. He'd grown his blond hair long and shaggy but there was no concealing the two brown lumps situated above the hairline. Carmela had once explained the difference between horns and antlers to me, but I couldn't remember enough to tell which these were.

'My God,' said Vanessa, and the young man flinched and gave me a reproachful look.

'You said you were *special*,' he said.

'We are,' I said. 'But some of us haven't learnt good manners yet.'

The young man looked at Vanessa, who gave him a brief professional smile.

'My name is Tobi,' I said. 'My friend here is *Kriminalkommissarin* Vanessa Sommer, but you can call her Vani for short. What's your name?'

'Gunter,' said the young man. 'Gunter Hirsch.'

I told Gunter he could put his hat back on, which he did gratefully. It obviously calmed him further. Once we were sure he wasn't going to bolt again, we let go of his arms and de-escalated from potential arrest to good-citizen-helping-the-police. They teach us to do this in training and it mostly works.

'How old are you, Gunter?'

'Seventeen,' he said.

I asked him where he lived and he pointed down the valley to the south-west.

'Down there,' he said.

'So, Gunter,' I said, 'why were you watching us?'

'Wasn't,' said Gunter. 'I like to come up here and look at the city.'

'Is that the only reason?'

Gunter shuffled uneasily and glanced back towards the Mariensäule.

'There's singing.'

'Singing?'

'Like a choir,' said Gunter. 'Only, you know, not really a choir.'

'An invisible choir?' said Vanessa.

Gunter gave her the same look teenagers have been giving adults since the first parent said, 'I don't get it. How can marks on a cave wall *be* a mammoth.'

'Makes me feel peaceful,' he said. 'So I come up here when things get tense.'

I asked whether anything weird had happened up at the Mariensäule recently, but Gunter said no. I prompted him a little bit, asking whether he'd seen someone up here more than once, someone who wasn't a local.

'No,' he said. 'But there were the wine-drinking guys.'

'Oh, yeah?' I said as casually as I could. 'What was weird about them?'

'Bunch of old guys,' he said. 'Having a picnic up here – they looked weird to me.'

A bit of gentle questioning later and we established that the picnic had happened two months earlier, in August and definitely on a Saturday night, although Gunter couldn't be sure which week. I took his home address and said that I'd be round for a chat later. This almost caused another panic attack, except Vanessa promised that we wouldn't tell his parents how we met.

'We'll say it's just routine,' she said.

When we said he could go, he literally bolted. Across the road and into the trees. It was extraordinary how quiet and light-footed he was.

'How many?' asked Vanessa.

'How many what?'

'How many *special* people. In the whole country?'

'Thousands,' I said. 'Hundreds of thousands, possibly as many as a million.'

'You don't know?'

'They're not all as obvious as young Gunter,' I said. 'You could have gone to school with half a dozen special people and not known about it.'

'In my school?' said Vanessa. 'I'd have known – trust me on this.'

'You were that nosy?'

'Where I come from knowing everybody else's business is a competitive sport,' she said.

'Where are you from?'

'Sommerscheid,' she said, and sighed. 'Where everyone is a Sommer.'

'Everyone?'

'Nearly everyone,' she said. 'And anyway, that's not the point. Surely we need to at least identify who they are?'

I'd asked the Director the same thing once.

'To what end?' she'd asked me, and now I asked Vanessa the same.

'In case they're a problem,' she said, which was pretty much what I'd said.

The Director had slammed her fist on her desk hard enough to break her coffee cup.

'And then what?' she'd asked. 'We keep files on them? Or why not make it simple and require them to carry papers or perhaps sew a symbol onto their coats. A scarlet pentagram perhaps. Would that satisfy you?'

'They're just ordinary people,' I said to Vanessa. 'Doing ordinary things.'

'And when they do extraordinary things?'

'Your boss calls my boss,' I said. 'And here I am.'

*

Jason Agnelli's phone was waiting for us when we got back to the Post Office. There was a terse little note explaining that the lab hadn't had a chance to run tests yet, so could we be careful not to contaminate any evidence. It was still in a clear plastic evidence bag and I picked it up and shook it. It made a noise like one of those rainmakers – like sand shifting around. The lab's data retrieval team wasn't going to get anything out of that phone.

Still, procedure has to be followed. So we got someone

over from K17 to take photographs as I took the phone apart and laid it out on a big piece of sterile white paper. Most people don't know what their mobile looks like on the inside, but even they would spot the fact that the main microprocessor set has been reduced to a fine white powder. To be candid, I don't know what the microprocessors do either, but I do know what magic does to them – particularly the type cast by a human practitioner.

'What does it mean?' asked Vanessa.

'We have an unregulated practitioner on our hands,' I said.

10

The Toy Museum

Officially there are only two active practitioners in the whole of Germany. One of them is the Director and the other is me. Before the Second World War there were thousands, but they either fled the country in the thirties or were exterminated, enslaved or co-opted into the *Abteilung Geheimwissenschaften* – the paramilitary magic wing of the *Ahnenerbe*. There was a whole secret dimension to the war that, according to the Director, had no overall effect on the course of the conflict.

'They cancelled each other out,' she'd said when she first briefed me.

The whole mess culminated in a British raid on the secret base at Ettersberg, which resulted in just about everyone dying on both sides. What the British did achieve was to get hold of all the *Abteilung Geheimwissenschaften*'s records, including a complete list of every surviving practitioner in occupied Europe. And what the British didn't get in 1945 the Russians recovered at the end of the war. And any practitioners who'd collaborated with the AGW, or at the very least couldn't prove they *hadn't* collaborated, were tried and hanged by the Western allies. Or just disappeared by the Soviets.

When the BKA was founded in 1951 the British,

French and Americans refused to hand over any records, so the KDA spent a fun couple of decades locating practitioners and either recruiting, imprisoning or retiring them.

'Retiring?' said Vanessa. 'You mean . . .?'

'They got a new identify and pension,' I said – at least that's what the Director told me happened, and she really had no reason to lie.

'Are there any practitioners currently in my area?' asked Ralph Förstner.

Once we'd informed Ziegler of the good news, we'd rapidly escalated up the chain of command to Förstner's office.

'Not that we know of,' I said. 'It was the first thing we checked.'

After reunification it became clear that the *Arbeitsgruppe Einhorn*, the KDA's counterpart within the Stasi, had managed to acquire not only the Russian lists but the British, French and American lists as well. These identified at least ten practitioners who'd been active during the war who'd successfully disappeared themselves into the general population – including, it turned out, into the upper echelons of the KDA. There followed a period of infighting and paralysis that continued until 2005, when the incoming Chancellor forced the retirement or reassignment of the upper management and appointed the Director as, well, the Director.

She was also, by that time, the only licensed practitioner left in Germany and the KDA was reduced to her, some non-magical support staff, Elton and his merry band and, of course, the Research Department. This was deemed perfectly sufficient to the KDA's responsibilities right up to the day the Nightingale took an apprentice and we realised history wasn't quite as dead as we thought it was.

I explained none of this to Förstner, Ziegler or Vanessa – of course.

The last estimate by the KDA's historians was that, in the time they were unaccounted for, the wartime practitioners could have trained anything between forty and a thousand new practitioners.

I didn't explain this either, but this time mainly because I suspected the Research Department had pulled the figures out of their arses.

'The glamour is not an easy technique,' I said. 'To make Jason Agnelli drink a litre of fermented grapes against his will would have required a highly trained practitioner and a great deal of "power".'

'Is that what destroyed the mobile phone?' asked Vanessa.

I said that it was.

Förstner was worried about the risk to colleagues, but I assured him that the precautions I'd suggested would be sufficient.

'Particularly if our suspect thinks this is all routine,' I said. 'When are the first of the interviews scheduled?'

'Markus Nerlinger is due in twenty minutes,' said Ziegler.

The rest of the Good Wine Drinking Association, Jonas Diekmeier and Simon Haas, would be coming in at staggered intervals. All except Uwe Kinsmann, who was not at his home address or work.

'Should we force an entry into his house?' asked Vanessa.

'Not without me present,' I said.

'You'd better get on with it, then,' said Förstner.

*

Uwe Kinsmann was definitely the wealthiest of the Good Wine Drinking Association, being in fact a gentlemen of leisure. His family had been prosperous and although he had studied law at university he'd never practised. Instead, he'd chosen to eke out his inheritance by living frugally and hanging on to the family home in East Trier. This was a pale yellow three-storey terrace, part of a row that backed on to the hills that rose behind the city. It had a long thin garden that let out on to a lane behind – this was our way in.

Because Förstner was worried he'd wanted to wait and bring a Special Operations Commando down from Mainz, but I assured him that was overkill. Instead we compromised and I went in with the local intervention team, which is basically a bunch of ordinary Pks imbued with extra training, each issued with a helmet, ballistic armour and carrying a Heckler & Koch. Thankfully they didn't wear balaclavas as well – a trend, according to my father, that comes from watching too much American TV.

Half of them waited with Vanessa outside the front door and the rest with me at the back gate. My half was led by Maximilian Uzun, whose enthusiasm for live fire exercises didn't fill me with confidence. Still, while we were waiting for Ziegler to signal the go-ahead, I did get a chance to ask Max about his name.

'My papa liked the sound of it,' he said. 'My grand-father had a fit though.'

Ziegler called us on the radio. 'When you're ready,' she said.

The garden was both neat and cluttered. Fifty metres long and only ten wide, it was crowded with a raised ornamental pool plus fountain, an arbour, and a white wooden rotunda that filled it from side to side. Uwe Kinsmann was either a keen gardener or he diverted a significant part of his inheritance to hiring a professional.

A large conservatory protruded from the back of the house proper and I tried that door first. As I touched the handle I felt the unpleasant wriggling sensation that had marked Jürg Koch's body, the malignancy in Frau Stracker's field and the Mariensäule.

I signalled the intervention team.

'Stay away from the conservatory,' I said.

I tried the back door, which was magic-free and unlocked. It led to a well-equipped but old-fashioned kitchen with solid dark wood cabinets, a lumpy white enamelled stove with rounded corners and a big farmhouse kitchen table. The room was clean but not sterile. The washing-up had been done, but a box of cereal and a sugar jar sat on the counter with a clean bowl and spoon beside them. There was an old-fashioned serving hatch into the dining room. I had a look – a large polished mahogany table with matching dining chairs and an empty sandy-coloured vase on a crimson mat in the centre. I passed quickly through a gloomily antique hallway into the dining room. There was a smell of overripe fruit which was definitely not a *vestigium*. I checked the heavy purple ceramic fruit bowl I found on a sideboard, but it was empty and smelt only of surface cleaner.

There was a connecting arch to the living room and a back door into the conservatory. Again there were *vestigia* at the threshold, so I left one of the intervention team on guard with instructions not to let anyone in.

It took me less than ten minutes to run through the rest of the house. The living room had antique armchairs with expensive floral covers and more mahogany in the form of occasional tables and glass-fronted bookcases. There was a modern flat-screen TV and Blu-ray player and an expensive Bang & Olufsen stereo system that dated back to the 1960s. Upstairs was the bathroom, which seemed blindingly white after the gloomy stairs, a master bedroom that smelt like someone slept in it, and three other bedrooms that were definitely for guests who were never coming.

There were no other magical hotspots, so I told the intervention team they could stand down and let Vanessa and Ziegler in.

'There's been some activity centred around the conservatory,' I said.

'Is it safe to go in?' asked Ziegler.

I said it probably was, but asked them to stay in the dining room while I opened the door. Vanessa sniffed as soon as she entered.

'That's the crushed grapes,' she said. 'Like Jason Agnelli's stomach contents.'

The smell was stronger inside the conservatory. A bench shelf on one wall held a line of potted plants and a wrought-iron garden table with a cream-and-tan marble top sat under the window. I touched the wrought-iron frame and the *vestigia* was so strong that the metal itself seemed to squirm under my hand.

'Ah,' said Vanessa when she saw me flinch. 'Then I'm not imagining the maggots.'

'Something wriggly, anyway,' I said, because you should always confirm a *vestigium* when a trainee gets it right. Otherwise they get confused. 'This is where he was compelled.'

If Ziegler found this conversation strange, she gave no sign. I wondered if Vanessa had taken a moment to brief her on what exactly we were doing.

'And that's where the crushed grapes come from,' said Vanessa, pointing to the far corner of the conservatory.

There, sitting on a layer of spread newspaper pages, were a pair of clear glass demijohns, one still full, the other empty but for a green slurry at the bottom. The newspaper and the floor were sticky with the same slurry and the pool definitely trailed towards the door to the garden. I heard Vanessa snap on her gloves and then she bent down to retrieve a round red object that had rolled behind a flowerpot.

She showed it to me – a rubber stopper sized to fit the neck of the demijohn. There was a hole drilled through its centre and the broken-off remnants of a glass tube.

'Aha,' she said, and squatted down to retrieve a blown glass tube bent into an S-shape with twin bulges along its length. 'The airlock. Lets the carbon dioxide out during the fermentation.' She bent down again to examine the demijohns. 'This is wrong. You only leave the pulp in at this stage if you're making red.'

I put my hand on the tiled floor and felt twisty, burrowing *vestigia* again.

'This is definitely where it happened,' I said.

'Does that make Kinsmann our prime suspect?'

'I don't know,' I said. 'But I'm declaring Uwe Kins-mann a potential infraction hazard. Nobody is to approach him without me present.'

'He doesn't fall within KDA guidelines,' said Ziegler, which impressed me because I always assumed that the local police never read them.

'I know,' I said. 'But we're definitely missing some-thing. And I don't want to take any risks.'

Ziegler nodded – *that* she could understand.

'We have our "play date" in half an hour,' said Vanessa.

'Let's hope Kelly knows something we don't,' I said.

*

The creepy mechanical village occupied a whole wall inside the Toy Museum. The model's main street and every window was crowded with toys rocking back and forth in repetitive mechanical cycles. Chimps cleaned windows and hedgehogs tended window boxes while, below, pedestrian dolls pushed carts full of pipes and a rag doll spun round and round on a ladder. The clanking of the machinery was so loud Kelly had to raise her voice to be heard.

'This reminds me of Mainz during the Black Death,' she said. 'Only that wasn't as noisy.'

The Toy Museum was on the west side of the Market Square, less than twenty metres from the fountain where we'd first met Kelly and Morgane. Upstairs there were train sets and toys from all over the world and from all eras of history.

Morgane had grabbed Vanessa's hand and dragged her off inside as soon as we met at the front door. Kelly and I wandered in, with the vague notion of keeping both of them out of mischief.

'So, when you were young,' I said, 'what did you play with?'

'People mostly,' she said. 'Sticks, stones, animal skulls. Mud is fun.' I asked about the mud, and Kelly gave me a funny look. 'Are you likely to get to the real purpose of our conversation any time soon?'

'Yes,' I said. 'But I'm curious about the mud.'

'You make a ball out of wet mud and throw it down on a flat stone so that it makes a funny plopping sound.'

'A plopping sound?'

'We didn't have a whole lot to work with in those days,' she said.

Morgane skipped past us with a blond four-year-old boy in tow. Vanessa stalked after her, pausing only long enough to give me a black look before resuming her pursuit.

'Tell me about your lover.' I said.

'Did *she* tell you about that?'

'She said you tried to make him immortal and it went wrong.'

'That's one way of looking at it,' said Kelly.

Morgane came back the other way, having now also accumulated a slightly older girl and what I suspected was the older girl's teenaged sister, who was supposed to be keeping an eye on her. As they went past I heard Morgane say, '. . . but they had feathers on really.'

Vanessa pointedly ignored us as she walked past.

'His name was Christian and he was the love of my life,' said Kelly. 'Or at least that part of my life. His family name was Stracker and his family was even more influential back then. In those days we hung around the Elector's court because frankly that's where the fun was.'

'Did he know you were a river?'

'Let us say he knew I was special,' said Kelly. 'He called me his angel. We were married by the bishop himself in the cathedral and we lived in a house near the island where you left the wine. It's underneath the new road now.'

Vanessa came back alone and looking much more cheerful.

'The nice old lady who runs the place is demonstrating her collection of wind-up antiques,' she said. 'That should keep them quiet for a while.'

I brought Vanessa up to speed.

'Did you really make him immortal?' she asked Kelly.

'Absolutely,' said Kelly. 'And all it took was the blood of forty virgins.'

There was a pause and then Vanessa asked how she'd been sure they were virgins.

'I raised them in cages,' said Kelly. 'How do you think?' She sighed. 'People used to be more fun. Nobody knows why some of us are touched. I'm a goddess, but I can't tell you why I am not mortal any more than you can say why you're not a donkey. But it's well known amongst us that if we love someone and give them our favour unconditionally then they can live long and happy lives. Perhaps even for ever. Or so we believe.'

'And Christian?' I asked.

'I had hopes,' said Kelly, her lips turning down.

'What happened?' asked Vanessa gently.

'There was another man who thought he loved me,' she said. 'A clerk in the Elector's court and a black-hearted sorcerer.'

'What was his name?' I asked, because that's always the first question you ask a witness even when the case is historical.

'Gabriel Beck of Koblenz and a fellow of the White Library.'

So definitely a practitioner, then.

'He courted me, and at first I thought nothing of it,' said Kelly.

Because she was the goddess of the Kyll, and beautiful, and the daughter of the Mosel the life-bringer and Rhine-daughter. Whose every step brought forth flowers and fruitful vines.

Kelly paused at a sound from upstairs.

'Were those screams?' she asked.

'Laughter,' said Vanessa.

'Then we're probably okay,' said Kelly. 'Where was I?'

'Fruitful vines,' I said.

'Who wouldn't love me?' she said.

And Kelly was gracious and kind and let such suitors down gently. And if they didn't get the hint, then a polite suggestion from a goddess is as good as a command from an empress.

But not with Gabriel Beck.

'He was like you,' she said, tapping me on the chest. 'All wrapped up in his own power. I could smell it on him like perfume on a goat.'

But Kelly was gracious. Have I mentioned how gracious Kelly was? She chose to deal with Gabriel Beck's attentions through a mixture of benign indifference and subtle avoidance. A policy made that much easier when she met her Christian.

'It was as if the sun had risen in my heart,' she said. 'I

138

felt I had lived through a long cold night and had arisen on the first bright morning of summer.'

'How old were you?' asked Vanessa.

Kelly sighed.

'Two thousand years, going on sixteen,' she said.

Gabriel Beck showed a similar level of maturity or, more precisely, a precocious sense of entitlement.

'He said Christian wasn't good enough for me and that he was going to save me from myself,' she said. 'I persuaded the bishop to have Beck arrested and banished. Christian and I were married that year and the next I fell pregnant. The first child of my own body.'

Ferdinand Tietz did the preliminary sketches for his statues of Methe and Staphylos that year.

'That's why the statue makes me look so round,' said Kelly.

But Gabriel was obsessed and returned to spread vile rumours that Kelly was the spawn of the Devil, who had bewitched both the bishop and Christian. He had warrants signed by the Chancellor of the White Library that gave him the authority to lay those charges.

'And you let him?' I asked.

'I would have washed him away. But it was my time and I had returned to my mother's arms for my confinement,' she said. 'And Christian being young, foolish and German challenged Beck' – she spat the name like a curse – 'to a duel for my honour.'

Christian was a notoriously bad swordsman, but even so the duel was to first blood.

'Would that the first blood had not come from his heart,' said Kelly. 'I felt him die even as I gave my daughter life.'

And when her baby's cord was cut and she was safely swaddled in the care of her grandmother, Kelly swept up the Mosel with bloody vengeance on her mind. They must have felt her coming as far away as Koblenz.

Certainly Gabriel Beck must have realised what he had done.

'He ran from me,' she said. 'He couldn't cross my mother or my sisters, so he climbed the highest and driest hill he could find. And there he hid from me. But I found him.'

'And which hill was that?' I asked, as if I hadn't guessed.

'The Markusberg,' she said. 'Opposite the city.'

'Where the Mariensäule stands?' I said.

'Oh shit,' said Vanessa, proving that she *had* been paying attention.

'It wasn't there when I did it,' said Kelly. 'I didn't tell them to put that stupid thing there. Mother thought it looked pretty, and I hadn't told her what I'd done, so she didn't know that it might cause complications.'

'So what,' said Vanessa carefully, 'did you do?'

'I sealed him up in the ground,' said Kelly. 'While he was still alive.'

It's an odd thing. When someone tells you something that horrible, your brain often takes some time to register the implications. When it did, I actually flinched away from Kelly. She gave me a defiant look.

'He killed my Christian,' she said. 'This was not a good man.'

'It's still a horrible way to die,' said Vanessa.

'Ah, yes,' said Kelly. 'You see, I fixed it so he wouldn't. Die, that is. At least not in the short term.'

As if that made it better.

I was suddenly aware of the clanking and whirring noise of the mechanical village. Grinding on regardless.

'Are you sure he stayed buried?' I asked.

'I have people keeping an eye on the . . .' She hesitated. 'The site.'

'For two hundred and fifty years?' asked Vanessa.

'There are people, families, with long memories who haven't forgotten their old allegiances,' she said, but then she shrugged. 'Possibly not that long.'

I definitely wanted another word with Gunter Hirsch, our friend with the horns, about why he liked to visit the Mariensäule. 'I like to come up here and look at the city' my arse.

'Can you remember exactly where you buried him?' I asked.

'I think so,' said Kelly. 'Why?'

'Because we're going to dig him up and make sure he's still down there,' I said.

*

First we had to carefully retrieve Morgane and extract her from the gang of children that had accreted around her. While Vanessa and Kelly lured her away with promises of ice cream, I assessed the slightly dazed museum curator and ensured that none of the children went home with Morgane by 'mistake'.

After her ice cream, Morgane was further mollified when she joined us for a jolly jaunt up the Markusberg, where she'd never been before, and a stroll through the woods to the position where, Kelly was certain, she'd buried the unfortunate Gabriel Beck. It was less than five metres downslope from the Mariensäule.

That done, Vanessa ferried Kelly and Morgane back to town while I called Special Circumstances and told them what needed doing.

Elton said that I'd have to wait a bit while he rustled up a digger.

'Unless you want me to use explosives,' he said, and sounded very disappointed when I said no.

Fortunately, two of Special Circumstances had degrees in archaeology. So three hours later we managed to recover the bones of a human male, along with the rusted remains of a belt buckle and a knife. The two archaeologists said they were amazed how well preserved the bones were, given the general acidity of the surrounding soil.

Vanessa returned while our archaeologists were painstakingly recording the remains prior to recovery.

I asked if there'd been any problems, but she said no.

'Although Morgane is trying to persuade Kelly to let her go to kindergarten,' said Vanessa, Kelly having learnt about this 'magical' place from the little friends she'd made at the museum. I said we could worry about that once we'd dealt with our immediate case.

'We?' asked Vanessa.

'Förstner made you the liaison,' I said quickly. 'So that means it's your problem too.'

'Well, don't look now,' said Vanessa, 'but *we're* being watched – again.'

I glanced over to see Gunter Hirsch watching us from amongst the trees on the other side of the road. When he saw he had my attention he looked both ways to check nobody else was watching and beckoned us over.

'There's somebody else here,' he said when we joined him.

'Where?' asked Vanessa.

Gunter pointed further down the slope.

'It's just a guy,' he said. 'I think he needs help.'

The slope was steep and covered in bushes and trees and sudden vertical drops. Vanessa and I made our way down very carefully. Three metres or so below the road, in a space hollowed out by an uprooted tree, we found a man crouched down with his hands clasped over his head. He was dressed in a brown loden hunting jacket and grey-green corduroy trousers – all of which showed signs of hard use. Hanging on to an outstretched root for safety, I lowered myself until I could see his face.

One of the things you get used to as police is recognising people from their ID photographs.

'Herr Kinsmann?' I said. 'Are you all right?'

11

Supper Club

Special Circumstances has an alpine rescue kit and rather than risk trying to coax Uwe Kinsmann up the steep slope, Elton abseiled down to him with a stretcher. I said Kinsmann's name a couple of times and snapped my fingers in front of his face, but while his eyes tracked the movement there was no other response. An ambulance was waiting by the time we'd hauled him up to the road. The paramedics gave him a once-over and threw him in the back. I rode down the hill with them in case he spontaneously combusted or did something else equally disconcerting.

I sensed no *vestigia* off him but human beings shed traces of the uncanny very quickly, so that meant nothing.

Trier has a big, well-equipped hospital with a helicopter landing pad on the roof and all the modern trimmings. After a couple of hours they declared him to be suffering from mild exposure, but otherwise un-damaged. His mental state worried them since, while he was definitely responsive to stimuli, he was vague and unresponsive to questions. They wanted to keep him in overnight for observation.

Given that we were equally vague as to whether he was a witness, victim or suspect, Vanessa and I, after consultation with Ziegler, decided to leave him there with the ever-enthusiastic Maximilian to watch over him. I also asked Elton to stay and watch over both of them.

It was mid-evening by the time Vanessa and I walked out into the hospital car park. I was tired but I wasn't sleepy enough to face the inside of my hotel room. And I was hungry but I didn't want another restaurant.

'Do you have a kitchen?' I asked Vanessa.

'What?'

'At your flat,' I said. 'Do you have a kitchen?'

'Of course I have a kitchen.'

'No, I mean: do you have a properly equipped kitchen with pots and strainers and cheese graters and stuff?' I said.

There was a pause while she did a mental inventory.

'Yes,' said Vanessa. 'Well the usual things, yes. But I'm not a chef.'

'Fine,' I said. 'Can I borrow your kitchen? I really need to cook something.'

'What are you going to cook?'

'What would you like?'

She gave me a sceptical look.

'Anything except chicken,' she said.

You can't always tell what a police officer's home is going to be like from their office. I've had colleagues with neat offices who live like slobs and vice versa. My dad has a picture of him meeting Helmut Kohl on his office wall and returns to a home with a framed poster from the late seventies with *Atomkraft? Nein danke* hanging in the hallway. Vanessa's office was full of papers, Post-it notes, and things printed off the internet, cut out and stuck on the walls with Blu Tack. In contrast, the walls of her flat were painted white with a hint of beige and, while I nearly tripped over a box full of framed photographs in the hallway, none had actually been hung. The furniture was worn and threadbare and, I suspected, had come with the flat. I would have said her place was completely without character except for the concert harp that dominated the living room. It was huge, like the guts of a grand piano that had been stripped down and propped up on one end. It was as tall as I was and, I decided, of limited value as a conversation piece since the only question it begged was *do you play the harp?*

'Yes,' she said before I could ask. 'But I don't enjoy it.'

I wasn't sure whether I'd misheard, so I asked her if she really didn't enjoy playing. I mean, the thing took up a quarter of her living room.

'My mum wanted me to be a harpist,' she said. 'I had private lessons from the age of five.'

'Did *you* want to be a harpist?'

'Not really,' she said. 'But I'm actually very accomplished. Not to a professional standard, of course, but I can make it do what I want.'

'But you don't enjoy it?'

'Mama went to a lot of effort and I am proficient – it seems a shame to let the skill go to waste.'

'That,' I said, 'is the stupidest reason for doing something I've ever heard.'

'If that's true then you really haven't done much street-level policing, have you?'

Vanessa's kitchen was depressingly normal for a young German living alone, in that the microwave was obviously the most frequently used device and the cupboard was bare of spices except for a jar of mixed herbs that had never even been unsealed. Fortunately, Vanessa's flat was located up towards the university where there was a Wasgau Fresh Market that opened late – so I'd managed to do a decent shop on the way over.

At least Vanessa kept the kitchen clean and tidy, and it had a nice big counter for me to dump the bags on. I unpacked the lamb, the oil and the rosemary. She had one good knife and a chopping board that was mercifully clean, if only because I don't think it had ever been used. While I chopped the rosemary Vanessa opened up the files she'd brought from the Post Office and started working her way through the statements K11 had taken from the surviving members of the Good Wine Drinking Association.

'Anything?' I asked.

'Not so far,' she said. 'But Kurt Omdale's fiancée is his philosophy teacher from the People's College.'

I mixed the rosemary with the olive oil and rubbed the mixture over the lamb steaks. They needed to marinate for a bit so I cleaned my hands and joined Vanessa at the table.

'I hope you like lamb,' I said.

'I'm not sure,' she said. 'I don't think I've had it since I left home.'

'You'll like this,' I said.

K11 had done a thorough job with their interviews and we had a convincing timeline for all of the members of the Good Wine Drinking Association for the last two weeks. The two crucial times and dates were the Thursday evening, when Jörg Koch died, and the following Saturday night, when Jason Agnelli followed suit.

'Shouldn't they have met on the Saturday night?' I said. 'Wasn't that their routine?'

'Jörg Koch was responsible for that Saturday's activities,' said Vanessa, paging through the documents. 'When he didn't contact the others, they assumed he was busy getting ready for the visit by his kids.'

I opened my own laptop and plugged in my master USB pen. I've run through three laptops in as many years and no longer bother even customising the desktop wallpaper. Everything is on the USB pen which, providing you remember to disengage it, doesn't get reduced to a fine sand as a side effect of magic use.

'Did anyone call him?' I asked.

'Simon Haas said he did, but the call went to mailbox.'

I read through Simon Haas's statement until it was time to fry the lamb and the tomatoes.

'I don't think the drinking club would have lasted much longer,' said Vanessa, as I wrestled with the total lack of a proper slotted spatula and had to turn my steaks with a wooden scraper instead. Once I was sure the lamb wasn't going to overcook, I asked her what she meant.

'They missed three out of the last six Saturday meetings, and two of the eight before that.'

But only one in the whole previous six-month period. Vanessa's theory was that the Good Wine Drinking Association had served its purpose and was breaking up naturally as its members settled into their new lives. Markus Nerlinger, who had been the original man in a bar with Jörg Koch, had been promoted by his firm and was being sent back to the University of Applied Sciences to take his master's. Jonas Diekmeier, Markus's co-worker and the youngest member of the club, told his interviewer that, ironically, hanging around with the old men, as he called the others, had made it easier to make friends amongst his peers.

'Kurt, as we know, is getting married,' said Vanessa. 'And Simon Haas has met the man of his dreams.'

I had the lamb out of the frying pan by then and was using the pan to mix up the sauce.

'Did the rest of the group know?' I asked, wondering if homophobia could have been a trigger.

'Apparently he told them this June.' Vanessa read off her screen. 'He said, "The others thought it was hilarious because I blew the most money on the strippers," he said. He claims he felt sorry for them— Your mobile is buzzing,' called Vanessa.

It was the Research Department at Meckenheim, who'd dug up a picture of the Staphylos statue in its undamaged state. They'd isolated the face and done some image processing before sending it to me. I emailed it to Vanessa so she could put it on her laptop and compare it to pictures of the Good Wine Drinking Association while I went back to the kitchen.

'It's not anyone in the association,' called Vanessa from the dining room.

'Have you checked it against Jason Agnelli's face?' I asked.

'It's not him either,' she said.

They say that in police work, as in science, a negative result is as good as a positive. The people that say that, says my father, have never had to justify the overtime payments to their budget review board.

'If the statue wasn't defaced to hide the identity of the original model,' said Vanessa, 'why *was* it defaced?'

'Anger perhaps,' I said. 'Envy?'

Having inspected Vanessa's kitchen knives and determined she was safe from any psychopathic intruders, I carefully cleaned the vaguely sharp one and carved the lamb into strips. She did have a nice blue and white serving platter so the final result – once I'd thrown in the tomatoes and cheese – looked better than it deserved to. You're supposed to use watercress as well, but no one ever seems to stock it.

'Do you think it's natural?' asked Vanessa as she helped me find the plates and place mats.

'Do I think what is natural?' I said and realised I'd forgotten to buy bread.

'This improvement in their lives,' said Vanessa, clearing space on the kitchen table. 'Five middle-aged men and one guy in his thirties, all miserable, all going nowhere, they meet up, form a club and miraculously they all turn their lives around.'

'Why not?' I asked as I dished the food out.

'Some of them I could believe,' said Vanessa, poking suspiciously at the lamb. 'Maybe even most of them – but all of them?' She tried a bite of the lamb and looked surprised. 'You can cook,' she said.

She was right. The lamb was practically melting in my mouth.

'I like to eat,' I said. 'And I like to know what it is I'm eating.'

'This is excellent,' said Vanessa.

'Thank you,' I said. 'And if it's unnatural, them all turning their lives around, then what do you think caused it?'

'Isn't unnatural your speciality?' she said.

While we ate I ran through the possibilities.

'Assuming for a second that the source of their good fortune *is* supernatural,' I said, 'it could have been one of our friendly neighbourhood location spirits.'

'Kelly maybe,' said Vanessa. 'But isn't Morgane a bit young? Does she even know what middle age is?'

'There's a whole library of books discussing whether location spirits bestow their favours consciously or unconsciously.' Perhaps not a whole library, but certainly quite a large section. 'That impromptu picnic after the theatre might have triggered something. And rivers are not the only features of the landscape that can have location spirits.'

'The picnic up at the Mariensäule,' said Vanessa.

'I'd say possibly but that was only two years ago,' I said. 'And their good fortune predates that.'

'So what else?'

'Houses, crossroads, woods,' I said. 'They don't all have anthropomorphic extensions, and they can be as nebulous as a feeling of unease or a strange sense of the numinous. The livelier ones are often mistaken for poltergeists.'

'Are these the things our ancestors used to worship?' she asked.

'Probably.' I once got into quite a serious fight with a Lutheran pastor over this issue, so I've learnt to be cautious. 'There's no consensus.'

'But our ancestors used to make sacrifices to their gods,' she said. 'To the spirits of the forest and the sky.'

I deliberately took a large bite so that all I could do was make a vague non-committal sound.

'What if Jörg Koch was the sacrifice?' she said. 'The price paid for his comrades' good fortune.'

'And who did the sacrificing?'

'One of the others,' she said. 'Or all of them.'

'Jason Agnelli wasn't part of their group.'

'Perhaps they wanted to see if they could use a substitute.'

'It's a good theory,' I said.

'And?'

'I don't know.'

Vanessa finished the last of the lamb and neatly laid her knife and fork across the plate.

'It can't be an immortal wizard,' she said. 'Because we found Gabriel Beck's body just where Kelly said she left it.'

'It might not be him,' I said, just to be thorough.

Vanessa tilted her head to one side and didn't comment.

'What else haven't you told me about?' she asked.

'Revenants,' I said.

'What are they?' she asked.

I told her as she did the washing-up. And afterwards, when she drove me back to the hotel, she was silent the whole way.

12

Climate Control

There are bad things in the world, and most of them aren't my job. But, of the things that are my responsibility, revenants are the worst.

'They're like ghosts,' I told Vanessa while she washed up, 'in that they're incorporeal. But unlike ghosts they can get inside your head and make you do things. The term we use is sequestration.'

Vanessa wanted to know all the answers that I didn't have to give her.

'They're very rare,' I told her. 'And their victims rarely survive. So good intelligence is hard to come by. The very powerful ones can affect large groups of people. Remember the riots in London a few years back?'

'Vaguely,' she said.

'One of those was directly instigated by a revenant.'

'Large crowds of people?' said Vanessa.

'Yes.'

'So was Hitler one?'

'No.'

'You seem very certain of that.'

'Some very clever people spent at least twenty years establishing that he wasn't,' I said. 'Neither was anyone else in the Nazi hierarchy as far as we can tell. Not even those directly involved in the supernatural side of the war.'

Vanessa was about to speak but then frowned and looked thoughtful. Most people react this way when I tell them about the Nazis. Would it be more or less comforting if we could attribute that particular part of our history to the supernatural?

I used the same joke that the Director used on me when I wore the same expression.

'We're pretty certain Churchill was a werewolf,' I said.

'Really?'

'Not really,' I said, and dodged as Vanessa flicked some soap at me.

'You think that this revenant has possessed—' she said.

'Sequestrated.'

'Sequestrated a member of the Good Wine Drinking Association?'

'Or someone close to them.'

Vanessa held up a coffee cup and inspected the interior before giving it an extra scrub.

'So exactly how did they make Jason Agnelli drink the fermented grapes?' she asked.

'Possibly a direct glamour, like Kelly or Morgane. Alternatively, some revenants are the spirits of powerful practitioners and can perform magic through their hosts.'

'So Gabriel Beck's bones may be in our evidence room, but his spirit is' – Vanessa hesitated – 'inhabiting one of our witnesses?'

'Yes.'

'How the fuck are we supposed to find someone who doesn't physically exist?'

'Very carefully,' I said.

Vanessa waited until I was packing up to raise the question she'd been dying to ask for days, ever since the moment I showed her a palm-light.

'Can I learn magic?'

'Anyone can learn magic if they have a teacher,' I said.

'Can you teach me?'

'It's forbidden,' I said.

'Why?'

'I'm not qualified to teach,' I said. 'Only the Director can do that, and she's not allowed to either.'

'Again,' said Vanessa, 'why not?'

'There are agreements,' I said. 'International agreements.' Vanessa frowned. 'I'm sorry. That's just the way it is.'

*

The next morning I got up early and combined my morning exercise with a run up the hill to the old Roman amphitheatre that overlooked the city. After talking my way in, I did a perimeter check around the top of the earth-covered stands before standing in the middle of the arena and shouting 'Are you not entertained?' in my best Russell Crowe voice. The underground area under the arena floor was accessible to the public and when I checked it out there was a definite air of feral excitement and the coppery taste of blood. Ancient *vestigia* rarely retain any sharpness, but the magic itself lingers and can cause what the Director calls secondary effects. We don't have to deal with much of this in Germany, but I sometimes wonder what it must like to be a practitioner in Italy, Greece or Iraq. Perhaps they learn to tune it out.

I ran back to the hotel and, after a shower, walked over to the Post Office and joined Vanessa in her office.

'Wiesbaden called for you,' she said. 'The residue in the demijohn at Uwe Kinsmann's house matches Jason Agnelli's stomach contents. Also, I called Kelly and asked what happened to her child.'

'Interesting – what did she say?'

'That the Strackers took the child. After all, she and Christian were legally married. So the child was a legitimate Stracker heir.'

'That means Jacqueline Stracker could be a direct descendent of Kelly's child,' I said.

'After ten generations?' said Vanessa. 'Half the region will be related to that child. Is being a goddess inheritable?'

'Nobody's ever dared ask,' I said. 'But it does reinforce the connection. And whoever or whatever we're chasing, it might have old-fashioned views about bloodlines. The more power something has, the less the actual facts matter.'

But the actual facts clearly mattered to Jonas Diekmeier, the youngest member of the Good Wine Drinking Association, who arrived for his scheduled interview a quarter of an hour early. He had brown hair, a square face and pale blue eyes. Dressed in a checked shirt and tight jeans, he looked like one of those men who had reached middle age in their teens only to realise their mistake and seek to hang on to their twenties as long as possible. He had that weird intensity, as if he were imperceptibly vibrating, that I've noticed amongst members of historical research groups and people from tech support. According to our files he'd been born in 1981 in Mainz and had moved to Trier in 2006 to take up his position at MSW Steelworks.

He admitted that until Markus Nerlinger had invited him along to his first meeting of the Good Wine Drinking Association he hadn't had much of a social life.

'You know how it is,' he said. 'You go home from work, eat something, play some video games or watch television and the next thing you know it's time to go to bed.'

He confirmed that the Association was breaking up.

'We all knew it. It had simply run its course. We would have stayed in touch, I think, but the Saturday night meetings were becoming a chore.'

He had been disappointed when Koch hadn't phoned to confirm an event last Saturday. Just because it was fading didn't mean the club wasn't still fun, and the meal at the Restaurant Eifel had been really good.

We asked whether he'd spoken to the chef – Jason Agnelli.

'He came out to visit our table and chatted with the others,' said Jonas. 'But his German wasn't good and my English is terrible, so he mostly spoke to Uwe and Kurt.'

It turned out that Jonas spoke good French and some Italian, but could never seem to get English to stick in his head.

'I know. Strange, isn't it?' he said.

We asked him if he'd ever heard the names Heinrich Brandt, our statue attacker and the assailant of the young Frau Stracker. Or Gabriel Beck, entombed wizard. But he said he hadn't and showed no reaction to the question. I asked him a series of standardised questions designed to elicit whether he'd been exposed to the supernatural without ever mentioning it directly. When I'd showed them to Vanessa earlier she'd asked why we didn't just come out and ask if they'd seen anything unnatural recently.

'You know what witnesses are like,' I said. 'Mention the supernatural and the next thing you know they'll be telling us about the time they saw angels at the bottom of the garden.'

But Jonas probably didn't have angels at the bottom of his garden, and probably wouldn't have noticed them in any case. He was obviously one of those people who basically ignore the parts of the world that don't interest him. The Good Wine Drinking Association, with its compulsory variety, must have been good for him.

We thanked him for his time, gave him a card with my number on it, and sent him on his way. While I wrote up my notes Vanessa finally managed to ferret out Heinrich Brandt's former address from the old case files.

'It's off Quinter Straße' she said. 'In Ehrang – so he wasn't lying when he said he could see his house from the top of the ridge.'

We asked K11 to see if they could determine who the current owners were, and set out for the hospital to see if Uwe Kinsmann was ready to talk.

Uwe had his very own room at the hospital, guarded by Max, who must have been racking up the overtime this week, and one of Elton's Special Circumstances team because the BKA were paying for the room. They went off for coffee while we informed Uwe of his rights and conducted a formal interview.

He was awake, bright-eyed and eager to help.

If only he could.

'I don't remember much,' he said. 'Or, rather, I remember some things but not others.'

Jason Agnelli had been at his house, Uwe explained, because he was offering to rent him a room.

'We got talking after he visited our table that first time,' said Uwe. 'He wasn't happy with where he was staying. He wanted somewhere with a big kitchen where he could try out new recipes.'

'Have you ever rented out your rooms before?' asked Vanessa.

'Never,' said Uwe.

But wasn't that the whole point of the Good Wine Drinking Association? To try new things? Uwe had invited Jason to come over to look at the house after his shift on Saturday night.

'That seems very late,' said Vanessa.

'I tend to stay up late,' said Uwe. 'Reading and the like. Jason didn't finish work until twelve most nights and he said he was often too keyed up to sleep straight away. I thought he was ideal as a first tenant.'

'Were you attracted to him?' asked Vanessa.

'Excuse me?' said Uwe.

'Were you thinking he might be a potential boyfriend?'

Uwe gave Vanessa a look of pure incomprehension.

'Oh,' he said finally. 'Right. I see. That.' He gave an apologetic little shrug. 'I don't really go in for that sort of thing.' A pause. 'Sex, I mean. Sorry.'

Which is a pity, because it's such a reliable motive. We moved on.

Jason had arrived at the house just after midnight.

'How did he get to your place?' I asked.

'By car,' said Uwe.

KII had done a thorough check on Jason Agnelli, who'd arrived from the UK without a vehicle and hadn't had time to acquire one.

'Did someone drive him over?' asked Vanessa.

'I don't know,' said Uwe. 'Perhaps he took a taxi?'

That was a tell – the hesitation as he realised he couldn't remember, and his mind created a plausible rationalisation. He was either covering a lie or somebody – or something – had tampered with his memory. I asked what happened after Jason Agnelli arrived.

'He looked at the kitchen first,' said Uwe.

The chef seemed satisfied that it was up to his standard, although he did suggest that Uwe buy some new knives. He had to be reminded to look at the bedroom which, after a quick glimpse, he declared perfectly adequate.

'Were you talking in English or German?' asked Vanessa.

'English, of course,' said Uwe. 'His German was terrible and I had to translate for . . .' He trailed off – frowning.

'Translate for who?' I asked.

'For Jason, I suppose.' He didn't sound very convinced.

I asked what happened next and Uwe said that Jason had been delighted to take the room and they were going to have a drink to celebrate.

There'd been no sign of a bottle or glasses in the kitchen or dining room of Uwe's house. I made a note to check the logs to see if anyone had searched the recycling.

'He asked me whether I objected to him having a woman stay over,' said Uwe. 'I said I didn't, and then asked if he had anyone in mind. He said yes, as it happened, he rather thought he was in with a chance with . . .' Uwe faltered and looked confused again.

'With?' asked Vanessa.

Uwe screwed his eyes shut and then opened them again.

'Jacky,' he said quickly. 'I remember because Jörg was so pleased with himself. Ever since he'd got back in touch with his wife he'd become very romantic. Thought everyone should have a soul mate but. . .'

He trailed off.

'But?' I asked.

'That's all, that's where I stop remembering. I'm sorry, I'm sorry, I just don't remember anything.'

'Calm down,' I said gently. 'You've had a shock and lost a bit of memory. It's perfectly normal.'

Vanessa gave me a sceptical look.

'I'm tired now,' said Uwe. 'I'd like to sleep.'

He lay back down on his bed and pointedly turned away from us.

*

K11 still hadn't determined who was currently living in Heinrich Brandt's old house, so Vanessa and I fell back on the classic police tactic of driving over and knocking on the door. The day was overcast and the ragged grey clouds were clipping the tops of the ridges and threatening rain.

'You speak English, yes?' asked Vanessa suddenly, as we crossed the river on the new bridge.

'English, French and Czech,' I said.

'How the devil did you end up with Czech?' asked Vanessa.

'I took it at police college,' I said. 'It's rare so I thought it would support my application to the BKA. How about you?'

'French and English,' she said. 'But my point is that everyone I know speaks a bit of English.'

'How else are we going to talk to the Swedes?' I said.

'Everyone, that is, except for whoever it was with Uwe and Jason the night he died,' said Vanessa, and I felt suddenly cold.

'Everyone speaks English except for Jonas Diekmeier,' I said.

I'd sat less than half a metre from him this morning and felt nothing. But that's what revenants did – they hid inside people's minds.

'Gabriel Beck kills Christian Stracker in a duel and is buried alive on top of the Markusberg by Kelly,' I said. 'Who then thinks "job done" and, still grief-stricken, gives up her child to the Stracker family to raise. Did she say whether it was a boy or a girl?'

'Boy,' said Vanessa.

'A century later the good people of Trier build the Mariensäule, which has the effect of channelling any ambient magic into poor Gabriel Beck.'

'You think he was still alive underground?'

'Alive, no,' I said. 'Conscious, yes.'

'That's horrific.'

'Fast-forward to New Year's Day 1945 and Heinrich Brandt, aged two weeks, is found in the ruins of his family's house. He was buried for five days and his survival is considered miraculous,' I said. 'What if that miracle was the spirit of Gabriel Beck?'

'How?' asked Vanessa.

'All living things are intrinsically magical,' I said. 'The magic gets released at the point of death.' Such as happens when the RAF drops a couple of thousand tonnes of high explosive on a town – evacuated or not. 'And there was a natural connection between Beck and the child, because of what they both had in common.'

'Being buried alive,' said Vanessa.

We turned off the main road and headed into Ehrang, which certainly didn't look any less dull from this angle than it had when I'd first seen it from the other side of the railway tracks.

'So was that guy Heinrich, or was he really Gabriel Beck pretending to be Heinrich?'

'I'm not sure, but if I had to guess I'd say he was Heinrich pretty much up to that day when he attacked Jacky Stracker.'

He called me 'my love', 'my beauty', 'my precious one'. Like a friendly dog who suddenly bares his teeth.

'Then Jacky shoots him and he runs off,' I said.

And then what?

'Perhaps he dies up there by the Mariensäule,' I said. 'If his body went over the cliff and into the forest he will never be found.'

'And then what?' said Vanessa. 'He jumps into another person.'

'Maybe,' I said. 'These things are rare and there's a lot we don't know.'

'Or perhaps he licks his wounds, bides his time and comes back with a different identity,' said Vanessa. 'Perhaps Heinrich Brandt and Jonas Diekmeier are the same person.' Vanessa slowed, looking for the turn-off.

163

'Diekmeier is twenty-nine,' I said. 'Assuming Brandt is still alive, he'd be in his seventies.'

'Not if the revenant kept him young,' said Vanessa.

I was about to say that was far-fetched but really, if the evil spirit of Gabriel Beck could cause Brandt to survive a 9mm round to the chest why couldn't it keep him young?

Heinrich Brandt's old home was half a double house on a side road off Quinter Straße. Vanessa parked ten metres short so that we could approach quietly on foot.

'Assuming either that they're the same or Beck sequestrated Diekmeier,' she said, 'why does nothing happen for over thirty years?'

'I think Frau Stracker might be the trigger,' I said as we approached the front door.

Judging by the freshly varnished wood trim on the door frame and the clean windows, somebody was definitely living in the house. Still, K11's inability to track down the current owner made us cautious – for all we knew, Heinrich Brandt was still in there nursing his bullet wounds. Which is why Vanessa automatically stepped to one side out of the immediate line of fire when I rang the doorbell.

Such precautions can save your life.

'So what are you saying?' said Vanessa, as we waited for an answer. 'That the spirit of Gabriel Beck rose up because Jason Agnelli took a fancy to Jacqueline Stracker?'

'Pretty much,' I said, and rang the doorbell again.

'That's way out,' said Vanessa.

There was a driveway to the side of the house and access to the back garden.

'Check round the back?' I asked.

'There's somebody moving around inside,' said Vanessa.

I banged on the door with the flat of my hand.

'Hello,' I called. 'Police. Open the door please.'

Magic is tricky and difficult to do. You assemble a spell out of components and that initial assembly creates a 'sound' that you sense in the same manner you sense *vestigia*. Ordinary people wouldn't notice it, but if you're trained it's as distinctive as the sound of someone working the slide on a pump-action shotgun.

'Down,' I shouted, and threw myself to the left.

There was a noise like ball bearings hitting a metal sheet – and the front door, most of the frame and chunks of the surrounding wall, exploded outwards.

Well, that answers that question, I thought. Dead or not, Gabriel Beck had retained his skills.

I rolled over and drew my pistol and covered the door as I scrambled to my feet. Checking right, I saw Vanessa take cover against the wall on the other side. Her face was calm but her eyes were a little wild. Police don't get shot at very often, so I doubted she'd had much direct combat experience. Still, training counts for something because she had her pistol out and was checking around to ensure we weren't flanked.

'Follow me in,' I said. 'And stay behind me.'

She nodded and I braced myself to go through the door.

Too late.

We heard the sound of an engine revving. But before we could react, a blue VW Golf flew down the drive, fishtailed on to the road and accelerated away. I caught a glimpse of the driver – it was Jonas Diekmeier.

Vanessa was already running for the Duster and I followed, cursing under my breath.

As we established it later, Jonas Diekmeier had been using Heinrich Brandt's old house as a second home. It was later speculated that the revenant Gabriel Beck had periodically seized control of Jonas's mind so he could maintain control of the house and the finances and have the occasional night out on the town. No wonder Jonas didn't think he had a social life. Gabriel was having it for him.

I arrived at the Duster in time to see the VW turn left on Quinter Straße and then had to hang on for dear life as Vanessa did a reverse into a J-turn and accelerated after it before I'd even got my door closed.

She slowed down as soon as we had the VW in sight. It's bad policing to pressure a suspect vehicle when you're pursuing it through a densely inhabited area. Most people will slow to a safe speed if they don't think you're going to catch up. Instead, your job is to keep eyes on the target while your control room sets up an intercept or a stinger team.

Only my phone was kaput. When I shook it, it made the faint rattling sound that indicated overexposure to magic. When I got Vanessa to hand me hers, I found it too was sanded. I hoped she didn't have any sentimental selfies on it. This is why I keep a spare phone, but that was back in my own car.

'What about your police radio?' I asked as Vanessa accelerated after the VW.

'Inoperable,' said Vanessa. 'I was planning to get it fixed today.'

We followed Jonas and the VW under the railway

bridge onto Niederstraße. Ahead was the jagged red-brown tower of St Peter's Church, and just before that the unfortunate Restaurant Eifel.

'Do you have a spare phone?' I asked.

'Back in the office,' she said. 'What's he doing?'

To our amazement the VW came to a complete halt outside the restaurant. Vanessa sped up to close the distance, but before we were twenty metres away Jonas accelerated off again. The Duster had been out of sight of the house and there was a chance he hadn't associated it with the police. So we kept the separation at twenty metres and tried to look inconspicuous.

The road curved to the right into the Kyll valley proper and Vanessa asked where I thought he was going.

'I think he's looking for Frau Stracker,' I said. 'My guess is he'll go for the winery next.'

'Then he'll have to go up the Karrenbachtal,' she said.

'If you can get next to him in the clear,' I said. 'I can stop his car.'

'Safely?' asked Vanessa.

'Just make sure it's in the clear,' I said, and didn't mention the high probability that the spell I used would wreck the electronic engine management of her own car. People get very sensitive about their personal vehicles.

Unsurprisingly, the Karrenbachtal runs up the valley of the Karrenbach – a tributary of the Kyll. Once you're past the built-up area at the mouth you're plunged into a shaded slot in the landscape. It sloped and was relatively clear of traffic, but Vanessa couldn't get the Duster close enough for me to cast the spell. I might have risked a fireball, but we don't cast them from moving vehicles for the same reason you never open fire from a moving vehicle. Not if you want to keep your job.

At the top of the valley, Jonas pulled a hard right on to an unmetalled lane that I recognised as leading to the winery. Vanessa closed the distance again – if he stopped, we wanted to be on top of him before he had a chance to react.

'I can protect both of us if you stay behind me,' I said. 'If he gets a shield up there's no point shooting at him. You'll just be putting us at risk from ricochet.'

The VW bumped into the farmyard. I saw some of Frau Stracker's workers staring as Jonas and then Vanessa and I actually skidded to a halt. Vanessa winced as she scraped the side of the Duster against the derelict farm wagon. I had my door open and was out before we stopped moving.

Jonas ran for the door down to the cellar and I followed. I'd have loved to let him enter and then barricade him inside, but there was too great a risk that Frau Stracker would be down there with him.

Momentum is critical when dealing with practitioners. Magic takes concentration, even for the malevolent spirits of the dead. For a successful capture you have to pile the pressure on, and never let them catch their balance.

So I went down the wooden stairs much faster than I would normally, with my pistol straight out in front of me.

'Gabriel Beck,' I shouted at the top of my voice. 'You're under arrest!'

I heard Vanessa following me down the stairs.

Gabriel Beck – or possibly Jonas Diekmeier, or most likely a combination of both – stopped halfway down the length of the cellar, next to the ranks of fermentation tanks, and turned to face us.

There was no sign of Frau Stracker, who I learnt later was a couple of fields away at the time. Jonas's face was twisted into a frustrated snarl while I continued to shout at him to surrender as I closed the distance. Then he went suddenly expressionless and I sensed him putting together a spell.

In a classical wizards' duel you're supposed to respond by guessing what the spell is and casting a counter-spell or riposte. The Director has made it clear that while she regards me as a promising pupil, I am not to engage in such romantic frivolity.

'We're not paying you to spar,' she said.

So when I saw Jonas's fingers twitch and sensed the weird twist that signals a casting, I aimed my pistol at his centre mass and shot him three times in the chest.

A Sig Sauer P229 is lighter than a P38, but any firearm discharged in an enclosed space like a cellar is painful and, literally, deafening. Even so I distinctly heard the buzz of one of my own bullets as it ricocheted off Jonas's shield and flew past my ear.

I lowered my pistol and flung up my own shield.

Just in time, because a fist-sized ball of lightning struck it at chest height and exploded – half blinding me. Gabriel Beck had been a master of the White Library and I'd been training for less than three years.

'Back up,' I yelled to Vanessa, and stepped back myself.

Jonas snarled and drew back his arm as if casting a javelin. I could see the air shimmer like a heat haze around his fist.

I backed up some more, but Vanessa stopped me with her hand on my left shoulder and her outstretched gun arm on my other shoulder.

I tried to shout *Wait!* But it was too late.

She fired once, twice.

A jet of water shot from the ruptured pipe above and behind Jonas, and hit him in the back of the head. It was, I explained, *at length*, later, a ridiculous thing to do. Apart from anything else, that jet of water could have missed, and occasionally I scare myself awake by dreaming about what might have happened if it had.

Still, it didn't. And the cold water had the intended effect of breaking Jonas's concentration. The spell in his hand fell apart and his shield started to collapse. I surged forward with mine still up and knocked him flat.

The water struck me in the back as I followed him down, but I wasn't relying on my magic by then. I slapped him hard in the face to keep him distracted until Vanessa got to us. Together we rolled him, cuffed him, hauled him upright so that he got another face full of water and frogmarched him up the stairs out of the cellar.

There were blue lights flashing beyond the gate to the farmyard and somewhere behind the painful ringing in my ears, the rise and fall of sirens. Someone, probably one of Frau Stracker's workers, had called the cavalry.

'Good work,' I told Vanessa.

'What?' asked Vanessa, mouthing the word so I could read her lips.

'Good work!' I shouted and she shrugged.

I waited for our hearing to return before giving her the lecture.

13

Recruitment Drive

Special Circumstances have a special prisoner transport van which mostly gathers dust in their garage outside Wiesbaden. It consists of an iron box with a complex pattern of enchanted metal welded into the outside. It used to be padded on the inside but they ripped what was left of that out after a practitioner set it on fire in the 1960s. The iron box is known as 'the bottle', as in *Djinn in a bottle*, and is currently retrofitted on to a militarised Unimog truck and painted black because some bright spark thought that would make it less conspicuous. It took four hours to arrive after we called it in.

Four hours of Vanessa and I watching over Jonas Diekmeier while he demanded to know by what right we were holding him. He was very convincing, and it's possible that the revenant spirit of Gabriel Beck had left his mind. Or, more likely, had submerged itself in the hope that we'd be foolish enough to let Jonas go – thinking him an innocent victim.

'But isn't he an innocent victim?' asked Vanessa, once Jonas was safely in the bottle with Elton himself as a minder. My hearing was coming back by then, although anything above normal conversation was painful.

'There are proper procedures. All legal and tested in

the courts,' I said. 'Once he goes into the bottle it's not our problem any more.' I sighed. 'As long as we do the paperwork properly.'

'There's paperwork for magic?' asked Vanessa.

'Not so glamorous now, eh?' I said.

Because there's paperwork for everything, except perhaps spontaneous river goddess creation.

*

'She wants to go to kindergarten,' said Kelly.

I'd gone back to my hotel to find her waiting to ambush me in my room. I didn't ask how she'd got in – no doubt she just asked one of the staff to lend her a master key card.

'It was the revenant spirit of Gabriel Beck,' I said.

'Really?' Kelly shrugged. 'Is he dead?'

'Taken care of,' I said.

'Fine,' said Kelly. 'Now about kindergarten—'

'That's it?' I asked, because her attitude seemed a bit too forgiving to be true.

'I settled that matter two hundred and fifty years ago, and since then my mother has become my daughter, and the German state has tried to kill me twice. But now it wants to be my friend. The world is turned upside down and Morgane wants to go to school.'

'Why not let her, then?' I asked.

'Oh yes, because that wouldn't be a disaster,' said Kelly. 'And when she puts the glamour on her teacher? Or has her new friends come round for a sleepover in the river?'

'You'll have to teach her to fit in,' I said.

'But how?' asked Kelly.

'I am but a fleeting mortal,' I said. 'You're a goddess with the wisdom of the ages.'

'Not helpful,' she said.

'How do your precious London rivers do it?' I asked, which for some reason caused Kelly to laugh so hard she had to put out a hand to steady herself. I waited patiently for her to stop.

'What's so funny?' I asked.

'You're not my type,' she said, and refused to explain further.

*

'Do you think she'll listen to you?' asked the Director.

The Director looks taller than she is because of her long face and narrow shoulders and her habit of wearing ten-centimetre heels in all environments that aren't active combat zones. She's very pale, dresses in red, and was currently wearing her hair in a bob that fitted her head like a helmet. She'd arrived that morning to debrief the upper echelons of the Trier Police so that they wouldn't do anything foolish – like hold a press conference.

Then she made me walk with her down to the banks of the Mosel, ostensibly so that we couldn't be overheard but truly so she could smoke her horrible cigarettes while she debriefed me.

'I did suggest that she set up a house near the school and play mother,' I said. 'Perhaps also volunteer as a reading assistant to keep an eye on Morgane – at least for the first year.'

'She could teach swimming,' said the Director.

'Not helpful,' I said.

'Why not?' said the Director. 'Nobody's going to drown while she's supervising.'

It was the Director's opinion that we needed the good will of the Mosel and her tributaries if only to curry favour with the Rhine Maidens who, so far, had proved strangely reluctant to talk to us. The Research Department were calling this new approach the London Paradigm.

'Perhaps the resourceful Vanessa Sommer will be useful in this regard,' said the Director. 'What do you think of her professionally?'

I could see where this was going, and I briefly considered telling the Director that Vanessa was sloppy, unprofessional and easily distracted. But this was not my choice to make.

'Intelligent and resourceful,' I said.

'Ambitious?'

'Yes,' I said.

'Then we must meet her,' said the Director.

But first we had to do welfare checks on the surviving members of the Good Wine Drinking Association. Uwe Kinsmann was released from hospital with no apparent lasting injuries, although he was unlikely to recover his memory of what happened the night Jason Agnelli died. Kurt Omdale, Simon Haas and Markus Nerlinger stepped up to organise the funeral for Jörg Koch. By all reports it was well attended and at the wake his estranged wife was moved to tears because she never knew that Jörg had so many good friends.

Frau Stracker provided the wine.

Papa had said that you were supposed to come home at the end of the shift to the important stuff – friends, house, hearth and dog.

One day I might have those things, although I think a cat would be more practical. But right now I'm having way too much fun.

Vanessa, of course, has her harp.

We met where it all started, on the lane at the bottom of the vineyard where Jörg Koch died. The Director was walking the burnt section to see if she could figure out where the malignity had come from.

'There's no such person as Jonas Diekmeier,' she said, as she bent down to sniff the ground. 'Our colleagues in OE think he was an entirely constructed identity.'

Abteilung OE did a range of activities in support of the rest of the BKA, ranging from communication intercepts to covert surveillance and armed interventions. Never mind where the bodies were buried; OE knew where the files were kept – much handier in a modern policing environment.

'So Jonas was Heinrich,' said Vanessa.

'Or was he Gabriel Beck?' I said.

'Not necessarily either,' said the Director. 'He may have ended up having multiple personalities or become confused as to his own identity.'

This was a well-known problem amongst colleagues in deep undercover operations and that was without the mind-bending possibilities offered by the supernatural.

The Director scuffed at the ground with the toe of the tatty Adidas trainers she wore when she didn't want to ruin her shoes. I was the current keeper of the good shoes and under strict instructions not to hold them by the straps.

'So which one of them decided to kill Jason Agnelli?' asked Vanessa.

'At a guess,' said the Director. 'A combination of Gabriel Beck for irrational jealousy and Heinrich Brandt's lust for Frau Stracker.' She paused to take in Vanessa's sceptical expression. 'At a guess. With any luck psychiatrists can unravel him enough so he can tell us himself.'

'Whichever one he is by then,' I muttered.

Vanessa nodded to the ditch where a stray yellow evidence tag had avoided the clear-up.

'And Jörg Koch?' she asked.

'His role as matchmaker,' said the Director as she climbed over the fence to join us on the lane. 'Or perhaps he stumbled into the malignity by accident.'

Like a man stepping on a vintage landmine.

Vanessa looked sceptical.

You wanted magic in your life, I thought. *Congratulations.*

'How do these malignancies start in the first place?' asked Vanessa.

'There are lots of theories,' said the Director. 'Very few facts.'

'Perhaps they're like opportunistic infections,' said Vanessa. 'The ones that occur when the body's immune system is compromised.'

The Director gave me a satisfied little smirk.

'Tell me,' she said, her smile turning predatory as she turned to Vanessa. 'Do you enjoy provincial law enforcement?'

'Say yes,' I said.

'It has its moments,' said Vanessa.

I shook my head.

'Have you considered a transfer to the *Bundeskriminalamt*?' asked the Director.

'Do you think that's a good idea?' said Vanessa.

I would have said no, but the Director silenced me with a curt wave of her hand.

'I think it's an excellent idea,' said the Director.

'Can I learn magic?' asked Vanessa.

The Director smiled.

'That depends on you,' she said. 'It's a serious commitment.'

Vanessa looked at me. 'You said the numbers were strictly restricted,' she said.

I looked at the Director, who shrugged.

'The embassy in London has reported that there are at least five active practitioners in Great Britain, the French have reopened the Academy, and Nightingale has another, junior, apprentice – who they described as "absolutely terrifying",' she said. 'I'd say the old agreements have been comprehensively superseded.'

I thought she looked far too pleased with the situation.

Vanessa did, too, but at least she had an excuse – she hasn't read the same files as me.

*

She came to my hotel the next day to see me off.

'You're really planning to transfer?' I asked, as I made sure that my flamethrower was safely stowed in the back of the VW.

'I put in the request this morning,' she said.

'Whatever else,' I said, 'I want you to remember that this was not my fault.'

She put her hand on her heart.

'I solemnly promise to take responsibility for my own actions,' she said.

'Just don't come crying to me when something with long claws tries to rip your face off,' I said.

'Has that ever happened?' she asked.

'No,' I said. 'Not yet – but it's only a matter of time.'

And that's where the case ended. Except for the paper-work, which only took a month and a half to complete.

Technical Notes

There is no statue of Methe or Staphylos at the Stadtmuseum in Trier, although given how many statues Ferdinand Tietz knocked out during his career and his obsession with Greek mythology there's bound to be at least one of them somewhere.

There are no and, as far as I know, never have been any vineyards on the slopes above Ehrang, and I apologise for the liberties I have taken with wineries and viniculture in the Mosel valley.

Trier is a fascinating city and well worth a visit. Come for the Romans, stay for the wine, and nurse your hangover with a nice cruise up the river.

Acknowledgements

This book would not have been possible without the patient help of Kristina Arnold, my editor at DTV, my German translator Christine Blum, or Antje Freudenberg, who provided much needed policing background. Also vital were Sabine Bamberg, *Kriminalhauptkommissarin* with the Trier Police, and the many Germans on Twitter who stepped in to answer what, to them, were some very obvious questions. Any mistakes, incongruities and downright moments of un-Germanness are entirely down to me.